FLESH AND STEEL

Marie de Cleves smiled with pleasure as she let her hands play gently over Draco Falcon's body. It was the most magnificent male body she had ever seen, a body as perfect as a god's, yet it shared the strange scar that marked Falcon's handsome face—a pale line that ran down from his forehead to his groin, almost reaching the manhood that Marie could see rising once more.

"Not again, my love," she sighed. "You can't be . . ."

Then, suddenly, Falcon's muscles went iron hard. He leaped to his feet and swiftly moved to peer out the narrow castle window.

"I should have guessed it," he snarled. "A night attack."

And Marie saw this man reach not for his clothes but for his gleaming sword as he rushed out of the room to nakedly face death—and to deal it out. . . .

THE FALCON STRIKES

Exciting Fiction From SIGNET

THE FALCON #1

THE FALCON STRIKES

by
Mark Ramsay

A SIGNET BOOK
NEW AMERICAN LIBRARY

TIMES MIRROR

For the Wolf Brothers.
Long may they ramble and howl.

 SIGNET TRADEMARK REG. U.S. PAT. OFF. AND FOREIGN COUNTRIES
REGISTERED TRADEMARK—MARCA REGISTRADA
HECHO EN CHICAGO, U.S.A.

SIGNET, SIGNET CLASSICS, MENTOR, PLUME, MERIDIAN AND NAL
BOOKS are published by The New American Library, Inc.,
1633 Broadway, New York, New York 10019

First Printing, September, 1982

1 2 3 4 5 6 7 8 9

PRINTED IN THE UNITED STATES OF AMERICA

ONE

THE trees hung thick above the narrow, winding road, and a light mist blew in wisps on the late-morning breeze. A pack of men sat encamped in the middle of the road, and there were horses tethered to nearby trees. All were armed, and most wore scraps of armor. There was a hungry, predatory look about them.

A runner came bounding along the road, and he stopped before the only fully armored man in the group.

"Two riders, Sir Ranulf," the man gasped.

"Armed?"

"To the teeth. One's a knight, surely. The other a man-at-arms."

"Are they heavy-lumbered?" Ranulf asked. Sometimes knights traveled with considerable wealth.

"Save for what they wear, all their goods are on a single pack mule."

"Well," Ranulf said, "prey's prey, and it's early in the day yet. Perhaps we'll have fatter pickings later." Sir Ranulf heaved his bulk of flesh and iron to his feet. He was as thick as a barrel, and in his long coat of rusty iron scales, he resembled nothing so much as a squat venomous reptile. With the black-rimmed nails of one sausage-fingered hand, he scratched at the lice in his scalp before donning his dented helmet and calling for his horse.

Mounted, he surveyed his little band; a dozen scruffy, villainous louts who cheated the gallows with every breath they drew. The only one worth his keep, Ranulf knew, was the Italian crossbowman. At least that one was a soldier. The men gathered around Ranulf, waiting for his words.

"Here they come," a footman said.

Two men on horseback came cantering around a bend in the road. They drew up short when they saw Ranulf, but the spot had been chosen well, and it was too late for them to turn and flee. Ranulf studied them expertly.

One was plainly a knight. His fine armor proclaimed that fact. He wore a knee-length hauberk of interlinked rings that shimmered in the morning light. Instead of the usual wide, elbow-length sleeves, the strange knight's were tightly fitted and extended all the way to the wrists. This was something Ranulf had never seen before. The man rode as if expecting trouble, for the hauberk's mail coif was drawn over his head and the veil, called the aventail, had been pulled across his lower face and fastened at the sides so that only a pair of flint-gray eyes could be seen flanking the nasal of the conical helmet.

The helmet was an oddity, too. Instead of the usual construction of small riveted plates, it was obviously forged from a single piece of iron, and its pointed apex was canted slightly forward. The nasal, narrow at the bridge of the nose, broadened as it neared the mouth. *Well,* Ranulf thought, *wherever it came from, that fine gear'll be on my back before the sun's much higher.*

Strangely, the knight carried no spear. At his side was belted a sword with an oddly long grip, and a formidable ax hung from his saddle. Behind the ax was a cased bow and quiver.

The other man wore a short, sleeveless jerkin of mail, and a tangle of blond hair hung below his steel cap. He wore a short, curved sword of the type known as a falchion, and he had a small round shield of iron.

"You'll have little save hard knocks from those two, my lord," said the crossbowman. He was a small, slender man in a thick leather jerkin studded with bronze bosses.

"Thay wear mail, don't they?" said Ranulf. "That's worth something. And their horses are good ones. What's that on the knight's shield?" Lately, knights had taken to painting devices or patterns of color on their shields, to make themselves easier to recognize in battle. The long shield that hung from the knight's saddle on the side opposite the ax depicted a bird of prey clutching in its claws a forked lightning bolt.

"What kind of knight carries a bow?" asked a spearman, puzzled. The bow was exclusively the weapon of peasants.

"A Crusader, you dolt," the crossbowman said. "Didn't you know that the knights use bows in the Holy Land?"

"Silence, you base scum," Ranulf growled. "What do you know of your betters? Leave the knight to me. Crossbowman, find a place to ply your weapon. I don't want that fine mail holed if it can be spared. Shoot him in the eye if he gets too rough." The crossbowman faded into the trees. Ranulf walked his horse slowly toward the two riders until he was within speaking distance.

"Greetings, sir knight," Ranulf said and grinned, showing blackened stumps of teeth.

"What would you have?" said the strange knight, his voice slightly muffled by the aventail.

"Only your arms, your mounts, and your clothes, together with the mule and whatever's on it. I don't require your lives. It's early yet for killing." This was a lie. *Two such fine, strong fellows will make good sport over a slow fire,* Ranulf thought. From his vantage point in the trees, the crossbowman could guess Ranulf's thoughts. Sir Ranulf was one of those strange, twisted men who took no

3

pleasure in women or even boys, but found joy only in the torment of other men.

"Well?" Ranulf shouted when the knight remained silent.

"Clear out of our path if you'd live to see noon!" the knight said.

Ranulf broke into a roaring laugh, and his men laughed sycophantically. Then the strange knight drew his sword. He did not touch his shield, but held the long grip in both hands. Ranulf stopped laughing and stared. The sword wasn't quite like anything he'd seen before. Unlike the usual straight, double-edged knightly greatsword, this one was single-edged and slightly curved, a little broader at the tip than at the hilt. The hilt itself was a great bronze crescent, and the pommel was a smaller crescent with its horns pointing the opposite direction. More than anything else, it resembled a long falchion. Ranulf was familiar with two-handed falchions; usually they were just crudely forged armor choppers made of poor-grade steel. The light shimmered on this blade in strangely rippling patterns of blue and gray and silver *Damascus, by the Rood!* Ranulf thought. He hadn't seen a half-dozen Damascus blades in his life, and those had been mostly small daggers brought back from Syria by Crusaders. He'd no idea a Damascus blade so huge could even be forged. The secret of Damascus forging was held by a few families somewhere in the Syrian hills who wedded steels of many degrees of hardness into blades that were unbelievably tough and keen. Ranulf lusted for the sword as he'd never lusted for anything in a life spent coveting and taking the goods of others. The damage that sword could inflict upon him never entered his head. Fear was as foreign to him as compassion or philosophy.

As the knight drew his sword, the man-at-arms did something equally odd. He dismounted. With a dexterous kick, he cleared his saddle and landed with his small

4

shield in his fist and his short falchion drawn. The short sword was Damascus also. Ranulf and his men boggled for a moment at the foolishness of the action. Even if the man was not a trained horse warrior like his master, a horse gave a man a platform from which to fight. Its weight and bulk could force a way through a mob of footmen, and it gave him the option of swift flight if things went wrong. Here was a man dismounting in the face of superior numbers!

"Madmen, the both of 'em," one of Ranulf's men muttered. "Killing 'em's a mercy."

"Take them," Ranulf barked. His men, sloppy as they looked, went into action like a well-drilled team. Six ran at the knight, five at the man-at-arms. Two men grasped the knight's reins from the right and left, for immobilizing a knight's horse was half the battle.

The knight moved. The long sword moved in a figure-eight; one loop to the right, the other to the left, crossing just above the horse's ears. The two men fell back howling, one missing a hand, the other with his face slashed from chin to brow. The other group closed on the footman, expecting easy meat. As they attacked, the yellow-haired man burst into blurring motion. He ducked beneath a spear thrust and gutted the spearman with a backhanded swipe of the short sword. Continuing the same motion, he spun on his heel and laid open the face of a swordsman closing from his right rear. His dancelike steps bewildered the attackers, and he used his shield to sweep blows aside instead of standing behind it to block them and thus absorb their force. A man swept a flail at his legs, but the falchion-wielder leaped over the blow and split the flail man's skull before his feet touched ground again.

Meanwhile, the horseman had leaned away from a spearthrust and swept the razor-edged tip of the blade across the spearman's throat. The spearman stumbled back, grasping at his throat but unable to stop the blood that spurted from between his fingers. Two more attacked, but were dealt with summarily. The horseman wielded the curved blade with profound economy of motion, dealing one precise cut to each opponent, and each cut ended with the blade in position to deal the next with no need for a windup or change of direction.

The footman moved to the attack and slammed the edge of his shield into the face of one of his two remaining opponents. The last, seeing his chance, jumped to plunge his dagger from behind into the falchion man's armpit, where he was not protected by his mail. The falchion spun in the man's fist and lanced straight backward into the attacker's belly.

Has the fellow eyes in the back of his head? Ranulf wondered. *Is this witchcraft?* He stared at the bodies of his men. All who still could had fled. Well, he'd seen strong knights take care of twenty or thirty footmen in his time; that was the natural order of things. He'd see how much the man's fancy tricks availed him against a fully armored knight!

"Look to yourself now, sir knight!" Ranulf bellowed. "You've had your morning's sport, now I'll have mine!"

Shield held just below eye level, Ranulf lowered his lance and charged. The strange knight awaited him, seemingly relaxed, the curved sword resting on his right shoulder. As Ranulf drew nearer, the swordsman stood in his stirrups and the horse planted its hooves firmly. Ranulf aimed his lance point at the stranger's belly and to hell with sparing the mail. When the point was inches from his body, the knight twisted aside in a move so precise and so perfectly timed that it seemed as if Ranulf had deliberately moved his lance to miss. On the return twist, the knight seemed to swing the sword with real force for the first time. The blade hissed in a glittering arc from right to left and Ranulf felt it connect with his shield. Expertly,

6

Ranulf turned his horse as soon as he was past the stranger. Never leave an enemy behind your back for too long. The knight sat regarding him, and the footman stood with sword and shield dangling.

Ranulf prepared for another charge and noticed for the first time that the top six inches of his shield was shorn clean away. He felt a cold numbness in his chest and looked down. Something seemed wrong with the scales there. With brief horror he saw the fine spray of blood burst from the widening slash in the scales. The spray became a fountain, and Ranulf toppled from his saddle, dead before he hit the ground.

Draco Falcon dismounted and strode to one of the corpses. He ripped a piece of cloth from the body and began carefully cleaning his blade, to which a few bloody scales still adhered. The footman cleaned his own weapons and then began methodically stripping the bodies of all valuables.

"Wulf," Falcon said, "have you found any . . ." He froze at the sound of a voice from above him.

"Stay still, knight." Falcon looked slowly upward. Seated crosslegged on a tree limb was a man. The man held a crossbow and the weapon was pointed directly at Falcon's left eye. The range was little more than ten feet.

"If you shoot me," Falcon said, "my man over there will kill you before you can brace that thing again."

"Perhaps," said the man, grinning, "then again, perhaps not. I'm very quick with this weapon, and there's a good bit of ground for your man to cover, and a tree to climb."

"Well, what are your plans?" Falcon growled. "Are you going to shoot me or stare me to death?"

The man in the tree laughed and lowered his crossbow.

"I'd sooner take service with you, knight. That was as pretty a fight as I've seen in many a year." He took the bolt from its channel and replaced it in the short quiver at

7

his belt. With an acrobat's skill he unwound his legs and planted a foot in the stirrup on the front end of the weapon. With both hands on the thick string, he lifted it from its retaining sear and, inch by inch, lowered it until the stout bow was relaxed. That done, he hopped to the ground and strode to the knight. "The look on that pig Ranulf's face when he knew you'd cut him was worth all the kicks and curses I've had from him these past months."

The corners of the knight's eyes crinkled slightly, as if he were smiling behind the mail. "How do I know you'd serve me any better than you did him?"

"I never took his oath. I got a part of the loot as my share, but I'd not have stayed with him much longer. He was a stingy master and his pleasures ran to torture instead of frolic. It's a tedious pastime if you've not the taste for it."

"This one seems a likely rogue, my lord," said Wulf, who was now standing just behind Falcon. "You'll be needing followers, soon, and good crossbowmen are hard to find, north of the Alps."

"What is your name, fellow?" Falcon asked.

"I am Guido of Genoa, master of the crossbow."

"Know then, Guido of Genoa, that I am Draco Falcon. I am a landless knight, so even should you rise in my service I have none to give you. I can offer you only a rough life, good lordship, and a fair share in whatever comes my way."

"I've a feeling that by the time I've earned it, you'll have land in plenty," Guido said. "If you'll have me, I'm your man."

Falcon resheathed his blade and held out his hands, a few inches apart. Guido went down on one knee and placed his clasped hands between Falcon's. He then repeated the words Falcon told him to speak: "I, Guido of Genoa, do take service with Lord Draco Falcon, and become his man. His enemies shall be my enemies, his friends my friends. I will defend him with my body, even unto the death. If he give me land, I will hold it for him at his pleasure, enjoying the fruits thereof as long as I hold by my oath. This I swear upon my honor and in the name of the Savior, the Virgin, and all the saints." Guido stood and Falcon embraced him briefly, then Wulf took his hand. He was vastly flattered. It had been very nearly the oath given by a knight to his liege. A common soldier ordinarily just swore to obey with no talk of his "honor," a mysterious commodity commonly believed to be possessed solely by the wellborn.

The knight removed his helmet and hung it by its chin-strap from his saddle pommel. He untied the lace that fastened his aventail at the temple and pulled the iron veil away from his face. He then lowered his coif, and Guido had a chance to examine the man he had taken service with.

Draco Falcon was a man of about thirty with sharp, hawkish features burned dark brown by the Palestinian sun. Except for his fierce gray eyes and tall stature, he might almost have been a Saracen. He had one striking peculiarity of appearance: His hair was glossy black except for a streak of white which sprang from his brow on the left. From the base of the white streak, a thin line of white, like a scar, ran down his forehead and bisected the left eyebrow, whitening it where it crossed. The white line continued down the cheekbone to the jaw, and down the neck to disappear inside the hauberk. Except for that, Falcon was a splendid figure of a man, with huge shoulders and a waist that looked small even in the bulky hauberk. He also possessed a mouthful of fine white teeth, a rarity worthy of note. Knights who had any teeth left by adulthood usually had a good many knocked out in training and battle. A full set of teeth was a sign of a cunning fighter.

Falcon took off his thick black leather gloves with their pointed iron studs and helped the other two strip the bodies. The thieves had little on them, but their weapons were valuable, as were any other objects of metal—buckles, bridle bits, cooking pots, and the like. Iron was a rare and precious metal, only a little less valuable than silver and gold. Most peasants possessed no iron at all, and one with a narrow iron rim to his wooden shovel was the envy of his neighbors. An iron-shod plow was the mark of a rich franklin. To the common man, a knight on horseback was all the more fearsome in being clad from crown to knee in iron. The mere possession of so much metal conferred an intimidating majesty.

They bundled up their loot and loaded it on one of the captured horses. Except for Ranulf's, none was very good, but they were too good to leave behind. Falcon gave Ranulf's mount to Guido, and they mounted and rode away.

Through the long afternoon, Falcon was mostly silent, communicating with his men in monosyllabic grunts and scowling often. Guido and Wulf fell back a few paces to converse.

"Our master's not one for much talk, is he?" said Guido, whose effusive Latin volubility had been rebuffed several times.

"He's a man of odd moods and whims, is my lord," said Wulf. "Right now, a dark one's on him. Another time, you'll see him laughing and shouting and singing and chasing milkmaids from one village to another."

"How did he come by that mark? The white hair and the line, I mean. There was an old man in my village with a mark something like that. They said it was made by lightning in his boyhood. He was called Jacopo Lightning-Struck and he was daft all his days."

"It's something he doesn't talk about," said Wulf, with a sobering glare. "If you'd stay in his favor, I suggest you don't ask." They rode on in silence awhile, but Guido could not contain his curiosity.

"What kind of name is Wulf?" he asked. Wulf was almost as big a man as his master, and he also had the dark-burned skin of a Crusader, but his eyes were blue and his nose had been broken at some time. Now he smiled, showing that he had lost only a few teeth, and those still present were strong and white.

"My full name is Aethelwulf Ecgbehrtsson. In the Saxon tongue that means 'noble wolf, son of bright-sword.' Draco calls me Wulf to save time."

"He speaks familiarly to you, more like a friend than a master. And you just called him by his given name," Guido said, puzzled.

"Things were different in the Holy Land." Wulf said.

"I never heard that lord and man became equal over there," Guido remarked.

"They did if both were slaves." Wulf said. That kept Guido silent for a considerable time.

Toward evening, Guido noticed that Falcon was swaying a little in his saddle. He nudged Wulf and said; "Is our master asleep or drunk? I haven't noticed him pulling at the wineskin, have . . ." But Wulf was riding up to Falcon and holding him erect in his saddle. Guido rode up and saw that Falcon was glassy-eyed and breathing hoarsely. The Italian felt his brow.

"He's afire! What ails him?"

"It's the Eastern sickness. It comes back from time to time. We must get him to shelter. The fever is followed by chills, then fever again."

Guido nodded with understanding. "Oh, the swamp fever. It's caused by the foul air of the marshes. In my homeland we call it *mal aria*. There's a hermit's hut not far from here. He's said to have the healing touch."

"Nothing will heal this sickness, but if the hermit has a

roof, that's help enough." Guido led them from the road onto a narrow path that wound deep into the dense forest. The trees grew here in almost tropic density, and the fading light grew so murky that the men had to pick their way slowly, and they had their work cut out for them to keep Falcon in his saddle. He was reeling drunkenly and slipping in and out of consciousness. The last fading rays of the sun were filtering through the trees when they came upon the hermit's home.

It was a bark-roofed cabin of logs and mud and looked as if it had grown from the forest floor. It might have been a habitation for elves or trolls, and a dim, amber light shone through the only visible window. Guido dismounted and pounded at the door.

"Holy hermit! Open up—we have a sick man, here." The door opened and a small, elderly man emerged. He wore a robe of rough brown homespun belted with a rope, and the crown of his head was shaven like a monk's. His only adornment was a plain wooden cross on a cord around his neck.

"Who calls?" he said, squinting into the darkness. "Oh, no matter. Bring the sick man inside." Wulf lowered Falcon from his saddle and half-carried him inside, while Guido saw to the horses. Briefly, Wulf described the sickness to the hermit.

"I've seen this sickness before," the old man said. "Mostly in men who've been traveling in the South; pilgrims and Crusaders and such. I'm sorry to say that there is little I can do to help. My poor herbs and simples won't touch this. The best we can do is keep him warmly covered and give him plenty of water. If it doesn't kill him, it should pass."

"It will," Wulf said. "I've seen him through sieges like this before. I'm surprised that you don't want to bleed him."

"Bleed him?" said the hermit with a chuckle. "I'm not

a physician or any other kind of murderer. This man looks as if he gets to bleed quite enough in making his living."

"That's true." Wulf said. At that moment, Guido entered the cabin, carrying the saddlebags. Wulf took one and opened it. From inside he took a chunk of blackish, waxy gum and broke off a piece a little larger than a pea. This he crushed in the bottom of a wooden cup, into which he then poured wine from the wineskin. "Do you know what this stuff is?" Wulf asked the hermit.

"I do indeed. It's the hardened juice of the Egyptian poppy. I've never seen a piece as large as that you just held. It is said to be the finest painkiller in the world."

"Like most of the good things of life, holy man," Wulf commented, "too much of it can kill." He took Falcon gently by the shoulders and sat him up. Tilting his head back, he made him swallow the wine. Falcon coughed a little, then lay back. Within minutes, he was in a restful sleep. As soon as he was seen to, the other three men pooled their resources and cooked dinner. Guido had brought down a hare that afternoon with his crossbow, and the hermit had a good store of wild foods from the forest. Wulf brought out his store of precious pepper from the East, and soon they had a small feast prepared. With flour given him by pious neighbors, the hermit baked flat bread cakes on a hot stone, and they all shared the wine. They took turns bathing Falcon's face when the fever was upon him, and tucking the blankets around him when he had chills. From time to time he muttered incoherently.

When the meal was over, the hermit went to his prayers. Guido would sit up with Falcon for the first watch of the night, then the hermit, then Wulf would take the dawn watch.

Wulf was shaken from a sound sleep and awoke to see the hermit above him. With a soldier's instinct for judging

13

the time of night when he is awakened, Wulf knew that it was not yet time for his watch.

"What is it?" he muttered, sleepily.

"Your knight has been restless. A while ago, he tried to shout: 'Father! Father!' But it came out as a whisper. Now he keeps saying something about 'the lightning.' I think that should he waken, it would be well if he sees a face he knows."

Wulf sat up quickly. He rose and went to sit by Falcon's pallet. "Thank you, holy man. I'll see to him now."

"I'll sit up with you. It is not yet—"

"Go to sleep, please," Wulf said. "This is something I'd sooner go through with him alone. He would prefer it that way, too."

Soon the hermit was snoring in concert with Guido. This was not the first time he had weathered this with his master and friend. He knew that Falcon's body was here on the pallet next to him, but his mind was many miles away and many years in the past. Once again, Falcon began to mutter about the lightning.

TWO

T HE two ships lay grappled together like mating
    sea serpents as the lightning sizzled around them.
The driving rain washed the blood from the decks almost
as fast as it collected. On both decks men struggled and
died in maniacal fury. From time to time a man fell into
the water, to be dragged under instantly by his heavy armor.

His back to the mast, young Draco de Montfalcon
stood, holding his shield with a weary arm and grasping in
the other hand a sword that was now notched like a saw.
The Cyprian pirates had attacked the Crusader ship as it
passed the island. Cyprians! Not Infidels, but supposed
Christians, even if they did belong to the schismatic
Greek sect. The Cyprians had boarded the Crusader ship
, at the bow, and the Crusaders had forced their way onto
the Cyprian ship at the stern. Now both ships were dis-
puted and neither side could break away and cast loose.
The fight had been going on for more than an hour when
the storm struck.

The winds and waves were terrible, but what terrified
Draco almost beyond enduring was the lightning. He had
never seen such lightning. Instead of flashing in glory and
winking out like decent lightning, these bolts were dim

and blue and they went crawling and hissing along the surface of the water.

"Father!" Draco shouted, "Do you still live?" His father, Eudes de Montfalcon, had been swept from his side a half hour past and was lost somewhere in the chaos of the deck battle. A snarling face appeared before Draco, and he hewed it into red ruin. The lightning terrified everybody and drove them to fight with a fury that was truly demented. Draco winced as a huge bolt struck the other ship on the mast, then jumped the intervening space to hit the top of the mast of the Crusader vessel. It slid down the mast and then went slithering along the yard twenty feet above Draco's head. The boy thought he would go mad. He hunched his shoulders and tried to keep his attention on the men before him and the lightning overhead at the same time. The lightning had one beneficial effect, at least. Men avoided the mast while it was decorated with the demonic blue fire. Slowly, the flame-serpent writhed down the mast toward Draco. Just before it could touch his head, it blinked out. But it was just an exchange of one death for another, for now three Cyprians closed in on the boy, their weapons streaming blood and rainwater and their mail sparkling with static discharge from the overloaded atmosphere. Abruptly, a hulking shape arose behind them and Eudes de Montfalcon was swinging his greatsword two-handed and roaring the Montfalcon battlecry, "Strike, Falcons! Strike, Falcons!" The sword sheared flesh and iron with the fury of his fear for his son. Draco was so relieved that he wept. Relieved to see his father alive, relieved to be spared death by enemy and death by lightning.

His relief turned to horror as he saw a gigantic bolt come sliding over the bow to go darting among the struggling men. It leaped from one point to another, here touching an upraised sword, there striking a helmet, then bounding over a knot of men and sparing them entirely.

16

Wherever it struck, men were wreathed in licking blue flame and fell screaming and writhing. It was working its way the length of the ship. "Father! the lightning!" Draco screamed. Eudes turned to see a man behind him incinerated, and Draco was spellbound with the terror that his father would be next. With idle malice, the bolt made a crackling arc above Eudes and flashed straight for the mast. Draco had time for a short scream before the world exploded in the brightest blue flash he had ever seen.

"Father!" Draco shouted the word and struggled to sit upright, but strong hands were restraining him. A blurred image of a face took form before him. Slowly, the blur resolved itself into familiar lines.

"Do you know me, Draco?" Wulf asked.

"Of course, Wulf, how not? I think I was having a nightmare, that's all. How far is it to the Alps?" He was struggling to set his memories in order. What was this place?

"We left the Alps behind weeks ago. This is the South of France. Come, do you remember this man?" Wulf waved a hand toward a small, dark man who looked familiar. Where had he seen him? Then the memories came flooding back.

"Oh, yes, the crossbowman. Good morning, Guido. Now I remember. We acquired you yesterday after the fight with that scaly lizard on the road."

"Not yesterday, my lord," Guido said. "It was four days ago."

"Four days?" Draco realized then how weak he felt. "Was it the old sickness again, Wulf?"

"Aye. We've had a time of it, keeping you from climbing out of bed and fighting all your old battles again."

"Where are we?"

"This is the hut of a woodland hermit. We brought you here shortly after the illness struck." Wulf turned to the

17

Genoese. "Guido, go and fetch the old man. Tell him the master's himself again." Guido got up from where he had been sitting and waxing his bowstrings and left.

"Wulf," Draco said in a low voice, "did they hear anything while I was out of my head?"

"Nothing that could mean anything to them. I sent them out when I thought you might say something they shouldn't hear."

"You're sure? Did I say anything about Odo FitzRoy? Or the Horns of Hattin?"

"Nothing, Draco. This time it was mainly the lightning again."

"Sweet Jesu," Falcon groaned, and his hand went involuntarily to the streak in his hair. "Will my mind never be purged of that?" Then his thoughts went to other things. "Who's this hermit? Another pestiferous holy man?"

"He's a good man, Draco, and he's treated us well and asked for nothing in return."

"Well, I'll not insult him under his own roof, but armed men usually get good treatment from those who have no choice anyway."

"No, he's not like—" At that moment, the door opened, and the hermit came in, followed by Guido. Draco eyed the rough robe and the tonsure with some distaste.

"Good morning, my lord," the hermit said. "I shall say special prayers today in thanks for your delivery."

"Your prayers I can do without," Draco said. "But I thank you for your hospitality and care."

"Everybody needs prayer, sir," the hermit said gently. "As for hospitality and care, it's I should be thanking you."

"Eh, how's that?" asked Falcon, mystified.

"Why," said the hermit, smiling, "since God rewards good works, the credit for this goes to me, not to you. While you have been lying here in a delirium, you've been storing up credit for me in heaven, and I thank you very much." Wulf and Guido were hard put to suppress their grins.

Falcon burst into laughter. "You're a rare one, hermit. Wulf, is there anything to eat? I'm starving!" Wulf brought a bowl of thick porridge made from barley and ground-up nuts and eggs and bits of fish. Falcon eyed it dubiously, then scooped up a load on two fingers and forked it into his mouth.

"Well, hermit," Falcon asked, when his hunger was a little appeased, "have you been pumping Wulf for stories of how we carved up the heathen in Palestine?"

"I've no interest in such things," the hermit said. "If you'd been baptizing them, I'd be more pleased."

"Just as well," Falcon said, "because it's the heathen have been doing most of the carving lately. You mean you don't preach the Crusade to the people hereabouts?"

"The Savior taught us to love one another, not to kill. He said to spread his word by teaching and example, not to slaughter those who are in error."

"You talk like no churchman I've ever met. I've seen fat prelates weep with joy when we told of Saracen children thrown into the flames. I've seen soldiers singled out by the priests as examples of shining virtue because they preferred sticking lances into heathen women's bellies to raping them."

The hermit shook his head, tears shining in his eyes. "To such a state has the church come. How can we ever return to Christ's teaching when those consecrated to his service counsel butchery?"

Despite his friend's attempts to make him lie down, Draco swung his legs from the pallet and drew on his hose.

"I was a boy when I took the cross, hermit. The priests came through our town, Cistercians commissioned by the Pope to preach the Crusade. I swallowed every word. So did my father. They told stories of the cruelties the Infidels performed on holy pilgrims—priests tortured, nuns raped, bibles burned. They had a big banner painted with a picture of Saracen horses shitting in the Church of the Holy Sepulcher. Father thought he could win grace by going. I begged him to take me along as his squire, and he finally agreed. I was fifteen. I was going to win my spurs and wallow in glory and be assured of a place in heaven by killing every Saracen I could find. We marched to the hosting with banners waving and set off south. Do you know what happened on that march, hermit?"

"I've heard," whispered the holy man, eyes downcast.

"The army must have killed fifty thousand Jews before we ever set eyes on the holy land." Falcon's eyes were far away. "It was the peasant footmen who did most of it. There was no way to tell them the difference between one kind of unbeliever and another. But they had plenty of support from the nobles"—he said the last word with a twisted emphasis that made it a curse—"and always the priests and friars urged them on. I saw a synagogue in Hungary crammed with a thousand people and set afire while priests called on God to witness and shower blessings on his people for their pious works." He snorted. "Rich sights for a boy's eyes. Father refused to slaughter harmless people. He even sheltered those he could. Even the bishops couldn't touch him for it, because he was the greatest rider and swordsman in the army, and was loved by many. But it earned him . . . enemies." Falcon shook his head as if to clear it. "I talk too much. I must still be light-headed." He lurched to his feet and staggered out the door with Wulf close on his heels.

The hermit turned to Guido. "There goes a bitter man."

"Aye," said the Italian. "Bitter, and proud, and I think a little mad. But he will be a great one someday. It's marked on his brow as plain as the white line and the streak in his hair."

"A great one indeed," the hermit said. "Poor man. I shall remember to pray for him."

For the first time since he was stricken down by the swamp fever, Falcon donned his mail. As always, he took a sensuous joy in the beauty and feel of it. Like much of his gear, it was of European design and Saracen manufacture. Like the usual mail, it was made of thousands of tiny rings interlinked, each ring passing through four others, the ends of each ring being overlapped, flattened, pierced with a hole, and riveted together. European mail was made of hammered iron wire, and all the rings were of the same size and thickness. This Saracen mail was made of drawn steel wire, harder than anything made in the West. The rings were smaller than those of European make, and their thickness varied throughout the garment. On the chest, flanks, and shoulders, where protection was most needed, the wire was thicker so that the rings were tightly woven. The wire was evenly graded so that on the sleeves, the back, and the skirts that hung below the knees, it was less than half the thickness of that over the vital areas, thus conserving much weight and allowing great freedom of movement. Any king of Europe would have been proud to own such a garment. It was far stronger than a European hauberk of the same size, and weighed perhaps a third as much.

After lacing on his padded leather aketon which went under the mail, Falcon picked up the rolled hauberk and thrust his arms through the sleeves. He raised his arms above his head and the hauberk unrolled, falling of its own weight over his head and shoulders, down his chest and over his hips, a rippling waterfall of silver drops that stopped abruptly at his calves. The mailcoat was split to the crotch fore and aft to allow him to sit his horse. Falcon laced up the slit at the neck that allowed the coat to fit over his head, then he fastened the square chest flap that covered the slit. He left the coif hanging down his back.

Around his waist he belted his sword and dagger, drawing the belt tight to transfer the weight of the mail skirts to his hips and relieving his shoulders of some of the weight. His studded leather gloves he thrust beneath the belt. He picked up his conical helmet and turned it in his hands, admiring its design. Like much Saracen equipment, it was cunningly crafted to turn the force of a blow instead of resisting it with bulk. Dozens of parallel flutes ran from rim to peak, giving it great rigidity, although the metal was quite thin except at the brow and temples. The flaring nasal was curved to cover the sides of the nose as well as the bridge. The whole construction was exquisitely tempered and polished, and had it not been thickly padded inside with horsehair-stuffed leather, it would have rung like a bell when struck. The few tiny nicks it bore would have been deep, ragged gouges on an ordinary helmet. Falcon slung it from his wrist by the chinstrap and walked out of the hut to where his men waited by their horses. The hermit was with them.

Before he could mount, the hermit drew him aside. "My Lord Draco, you are a hard man, but the times are hard and have made you such. I think that within you are the makings of a good man. I wish to give you this." He held out a lead medallion rather like a pilgrim's badge. It dangled from a plain leather thong and was inscribed with the likeness of a lamb.

"What does this mean?" Falcon asked.

"This is the secret sign of the Order of Light."

"I've never heard of it," Falcon said, mystified.

"There are others like me, my lord. Men and women who want to bring about an end to the savagery of these miserable times we live in. Few are churchmen, some are

22

not even Christians. If someone speaks to you of lambs and winter, in whatever context, show him this. If he shows you its like, he will extend to you whatever aid he can."

Falcon took the medal and thrust it into his purse. "I thank you. I will accept this, but I can't accept your ideals. I've seen too much. Men are killing animals. They always have been and always will be. If I am any better, it is only that I make war on other fighting men instead of on peaceful people."

"In this age," the hermit commented, "even that is a great improvement."

Before making his final farewells, Falcon reached into a saddlebag and drew out a lump of the poppy gum the size of a child's fist. This he handed to the hermit. "Here," he said. "You may have a use for this."

The hermit took it and looked at it in wonder. "I thank you, my lord! With this I can relieve the suffering of many."

"Save a bit for yourself," Falcon cautioned. "At the end, it eases the way into the next life."

"I shall be content to accept whatever end God sends me. Go with God, my friends."

"I don't think God would want to go with me," Falcon said. He wheeled his horse and led the way back toward the road.

Guido watched his master nervously. He'd fallen into another of his dark moods this morning. They were three days from the hermit's hut and Falcon was fully recovered from his bout with the *mal aria*, but he rode brooding, with his head down. Guido was glad that they would be reaching a town soon, for the master was cursed poor company in this mood.

As Falcon rode, the monotonous clopping of his mount's hooves set up a half-conscious rhythm in his mind, and the rhythm formed itself into a series of names, endlessly repeated; Valdemar . . . de Beaumont . . . Edgehill . . . FitzRoy . . . Valdemar . . . de Beaumont . . . Edgehill . . . FitzRoy. Each name was a bloody lash across his back, more painful than the black, plaited whip of crocodile hide the overseer in the Turkish galley had wielded. He remembered killing the overseer, and he smiled, his humor somwhat restored for the first time that morning.

The town was called St. Rémy, and as the riders entered the city gates, they saw that a fair was being held within. Jugglers and tumblers vied for the attention of the crowds, and small bands with musical instruments had impromptu concerts going in a dozen locations. On a jerrybuilt stage, the members of some guild were performing a mystery play, while a group of traveling players were drawing a much larger crowd with an uproariously obscene farce performed on the back of a haywagon. From the church steps a priest was drawing the smallest crowd of all with a harangue on the evils of vanity. Children played among the open sewers and the heaps of ordure, and it seemed as if every available space that was not occupied by a human being contained at least one horse, pig, goat, dog, or chicken.

After the long journey through the forest and the open countryside, the noise was deafening and the stench was beyond belief, but the all-pervasive air of merriment was infectious. They set out to find an inn where they could have their horses and gear cared for while they joined the uproar.

As they progressed beneath the huge, overhanging signs that spanned the narrow streets, a man's eyes locked on Falcon from the window of a pothouse. "I know that one," the man muttered. The potboy next to him tried to catch the words. The foreigner spoke with the barbarous

24

accent of Ireland. "I know that one from long ago," he half whispered.

"Your pardon, sir? Did you say something?" The boy stepped back from the glare on the man's frightening face. The face had been ugly even before an ax or sword had scarred it hideously. A cut across the lips had healed jaggedly and unevenly, leaving the mouth permanently twisted half-open, showing wide-gapped teeth. Another scar divided the nose nearly in two and had taken a notch from one eyelid. He had only one ear. "Just pour me some more ale, boy, or I'll give you the back of me fist." He raised his tankard to his lips and stared broodingly at the back of the mailed rider. He saw the men stop before an inn just down the street, and his lips writhed into what might have been a smile.

As soon as they had accounts settled with the innkeeper, the three travelers set out toward the town square to enjoy the fair. Guido marveled at the change in Falcon. The brooding demon of this morning had disappeared, replaced by a laughing, mischievous rogue who seemed at least ten years younger. A busty wench peddling wine stepped in front of him, and he held the wineskin aloft, directing the amber stream into his mouth. When he seemed to be soaking up the wine overlong, she punched him in the stomach. He sprayed wine over her and himself, and when he caught his breath he tossed the skin back to her. When she reached up to catch it, he gave her plump breasts a squeeze, then slapped her on the rump. Her dancing eyes followed him as he made his way farther into the crowd.

They came to a clearing in the mob. Inside, a bear danced on a leash at the commands of a whip-wielding man. Falcon caught sight of a tall woman on the far side of the ring of watchers. She was a beauty, highborn to judge by her dress, wearing a close-fitting gown that showed a generous figure, her oval face with its fine fea-

25

tures framed by a wimple that covered her hair and throat. Her clothes were of rich velvet dyed with one of the new purples that were coming in from the Holy Land. There had been a time when noble ladies were seldom seen in public like this, but now, with so many husbands off Crusading, half the castles and townhouses in Europe were run by women.

The bear tired, and its handler began flogging it cruelly. Blood soaked its back, covering the lacing of old scars that showed through the fur of its back. With a bawling cry, the bear broke its leash and charged for the crowd. Before the horrified people could begin to run, the bear clawed two men and bit a third. Falcon saw the noblewoman knocked to the ground by the mob in its frenzy to get away, saw the bear running toward her, and took action. The bear reared on its hind legs over the terrified woman, and she opened her mouth to scream. In three great bounds, Falcon was behind the bear, swinging his massive fist. Under the blow of the ironlike knuckles, the bear's neck snapped as easily as a chicken's, and the beast fell dead across the lady's legs. Falcon, aided by Wulf, hauled the dead animal off her and helped the lady to her feet.

"You have saved my life, sir," she said, regaining her composure quickly. "May I have the honor of knowing your name?"

"The honor shall be mine, my lady," said Falcon, slipping easily from his usual soldier's patois into the courtly French of the highborn. "Know, then, that I am—" At this, he was interrupted by a tug at his sleeve. It was the bearkeeper, and he was furious.

"My bear! You've killed my bear! Now I have nothing! Who's going to pay for my bear?"

Falcon wrapped his bear-killing fist in the front of the man's coat and lifted him several inches from the ground.

"If you'd not tormented the beast it wouldn't have attacked. I've put it from its suffering, and I'd as lief do the same for you." He flung the man from him, and the bearkeeper crashed into the wheel of a cart twenty feet away, hard enough to crack two spokes. The carter began tearing his hair. "My wheel! My wheel!" Falcon tossed him a silver coin. "There. That'll pay the wheelwright for new spokes and keep you drunk for the rest of the day."

The man bit the coin and smiled.

"As I was saying, I am Draco Falcon, formerly a Crusader, now a knight-errant." Knights-errant, masterless men with swords for hire, were another consequence of so many men of rank being killed or absent on a semipermanent basis in the Crusades.

"I am Marie de Cleves, chatelaine of La Roche."

"Chatelaine in your husband's absence?" Falcon asked.

"My father's. He lies in a Saracen prison. May I speak with you in private?"

"Why, certainly," Falcon said, intrigued. "Are your lodgings nearby?"

"I have a townhouse two streets away, in the goldsmith's quarter across from the Church of the Holy Ghost. We can speak there." Falcon gave Wulf and Guido some money and bade them enjoy themselves while he accompanied the lady to her home. The men did not bother to hide their nudges and winks, but the lady affected not to notice.

The townhouse was a fine one, and its emptiness was a relief after the overcrowding of the town and inn, but Falcon did not fail to notice that the furnishings were spare and plain, as if the lady had fallen on hard times. She gestured to a windowseat, and he sat and watched her as she poured red wine from a pitcher into plain pottery cups. She moved with grace and surety, and her spine was erect as a spearshaft. Young girls of noble birth were trained in deportment by strapping planks to their backs and balancing weights atop their heads and were never allowed to sit in a chair with a back before marriage. Her dress exposed only her face and hands, but the tight fit of her gown revealed the proud jut of her breasts and the smallness of her waist as plainly as if she had been naked. She handed a cup to Falcon and sat on the windowseat opposite him. Her back stayed at least an inch clear of the wall behind her.

"You tell me, sir, that you are a knight-errant. You own to no master. Does that mean, therefore, that you and your men are . . . for hire?" She was hesitant to use the word "hire," with good reason. For so long had military service been solely a matter of feudal duty that the word had disreputable connotations, and put the knight on the level of the hired laborer. The very concept of a masterless knight was so new that it was almost a contradiction in terms. A knight was, by definition, a man who served his lord.

"We are, my lady. You needn't fear to use the word. Half the knights in the Holy Land serve some master for pay, after the liege they came over with is killed or goes home before they are ready. Are you in need of armed men?"

"Very much so. I mentioned to you that my father is held prisoner by the infidels. I have sold most of what I have to raise his ransom. With five hundred more gold ducats, his captor says he will release Father to come home and raise the rest, and give him five years to raise it. I don't know whether to believe him or not, but I have no choice."

"You may believe it. The Saracens are devious in many things, but they are always scrupulous about ransom terms."

"Anyway, Father's cousin, Thibaut de Cleves, holds the land and castle next to ours. He claims that I am going to pawn the land to the Jews to raise Father's ransom, and that the land will pass out of the family. I would never do that, of course. Father would behead me when he returned if I did. It is just Thibaut's excuse to send his soldiers to take La Roche. He has always coveted it, and he hates Father, me, and all the rest of our branch of the family. I must confess, more de Cleveses have probably been killed by other de Cleveses than by all their other enemies combined." Falcon nodded. It was the same story everywhere. Fratricidal feud was the rule rather than the exception.

"How many men-at-arms have you?" Falcon asked.

"Just a few old men and boys. All the able-bodied young men took the cross with Father."

"And Thibaut? How many has he?"

"At least two hundred. His fief of Pierre Noir holds six knights' fees, and he keeps every peasant on the place armed. He's taken two small fiefs nearby by force of arms, while their masters were in the Holy Land. Of course, it's forbidden under pain of excommunication to attack the land of a man on Crusade, but our archbishop is not above taking bribes."

"Few archbishops are," Falcon muttered.

"Thibaut has tried everything to gain control of La Roche short of using force. He has asked for my hand in marriage, for instance."

"It strikes me, my lady, that that might be your best course."

"Much as I detest him, I considered it seriously. But I know that as soon as La Roche was in his hands, Thibaut would cut off Father's ransom payments. He would probably send someone to do away with him, in fact. Sir Draco, I need help desperately."

Now comes the difficult part, Falcon thought. "My lady, I sympathize with your plight. I assure you that I understand your devotion to your father. But I only have the two men you saw with me. To defend your castle, I would need to hire many more. You have sold everything to raise your father's ransom." He gestured toward the walls, where pale square patches bespoke tapestries that had been taken down. "How can you pay for their keep, when you are still short five hundred ducats to buy his freedom?"

She looked down with the embarrassment of a noble-woman who was forced to bicker about the base subject of money. "I can feed them. There should be loot if they defeat Thibaut."

Falcon shook his head and said, "My lady, soldiers need more than that. There may be many months of inaction. If we could attack immediately, it might be different, but with the local clergy on his side, we must wait until he attacks, so time is on his side. As their lord, I owe a duty to my men, no matter how baseborn. If I contract for service for them, I must be able to promise regular pay as well as provisions and shelter. I am sorry." He set his cup on the windowseat and rose to leave.

"Sir Draeo," she said, not meeting his eyes, "I am still a young woman, and not uncomely." She gathered her courage and looked him straight in the eyes. "I would rather share the bed of an honest warrior in sin than accept honorable marriage with a sneaking, cowardly toad like Thibault. If you will help me I am yours while you are in my service."

Falcon was sorely tempted. The woman was undeniably beautiful. But in becoming a leader of men, even in a small way, he had taken up a burden.

"I am sorry, my lady," he said, and he turned and walked out. He did not want to look back at her.

The streets were still festive, but Falcon had no taste for their antics now. He was grim-faced and somber as he made his way back to the inn. The room he had paid for was empty when he pushed through the door. Apparently Wulf and Guido were still celebrating somewhere. He pushed the door shut and realized he was not alone. He jumped across the straw-covered floor and whirled as he drew his sword, placing his back to the wall. The man behind the door slowly emerged. In the dim light that filtered through the narrow window, Falcon began to make out the features of a hulking man, terribly scarred.

"Speak quickly if you want to live," Falcon hissed.

"So, you still have the blade old Suleiman gave you, Draco?" The thick Irish accent told Falcon more than the dimly seen scarred face.

"Donal MacFergus!" With a whoop, Falcon dropped the sword and leaped across the room, sweeping the ugly man up in his arms.

"I thought you dead years ago, Donal. Come down to the common room—I've nothing to offer you here." He bustled the Irishman down the stairs and into the packed room, where they shoved three drunks and a dog from a bench and seated themselves at a long table. A half-dozen chickens were roosting on a beam overhead and further decorating the already messy table, so they shooed them away, too.

The serving girls brought them ale and big bread trenchers which they heaped with cheese and sausages and onions to stay their appetites while the meats requiring more preparation were being dressed. Donal demanded a roast chicken, and one of the wenches snatched a plump hen from a table and wrung its neck. "Good thing you didn't ask for roast boar," Falcon commented. They set their teeth to the appetizers while Donal regaled Falcon with the tale of his adventures since they had parted company in Palestine. Most of it was plainly lies of the most outrageous Irish sort, but the tale was entertaining.

They were setting into the venison Falcon had ordered, carving off hunks of dripping meat with their daggers and stuffing the scorching flesh into their mouths, when Wulf and Guido arrived, each with an arm around a plump girl.

With so many men off Crusading, free women were everywhere. Wulf fell into Donal's arms and there was much mutual exchange of greetings, then Guido had to be introduced to the Irishman. By the time all the introductions had been made and stories of adventures since parting brought up to date, most of the others in the common room were snoring at the benches or under the tables. The men felt the need of a little something more to soak up all the ale and wine they were drinking, so the girls went back to the kitchen to see what they could wheedle from the cook.

They returned with a huge meat pie, which the cook had given them because the party of merchants who had ordered it had all passed out before it finished baking.

"Now, this is a dish worthy to top off our evening," Wulf said. With the pommel of his dagger, he smashed in the top crust, releasing a savory steam which set their mouths to watering in spite of the huge amounts they had already eaten and drunk. They were all old soldiers, accustomed to starving for long periods when necessary, then gorging enormously when plenty of food and drink were available. From the interior of the pie, they speared out partridges, chunks of boar, kidneys, a lobster, beef ribs, and several things which nobody at the table could identify, but which were delicious anyway.

When all but small scraps of the meat was gone, one of the women gathered up the pie crust and everything else that was edible and carried it to the door, where a gang of beggars was waiting, under the direction of the local beggar king, to be doled out their share of their betters' food. The gravy-soaked bread trenchers were a special favorite, but the beggar king made sure that there were no fights in which precious food might be spilled and wasted.

Falcon and Donal staggered up the stairs, heavy-bellied, arms around each other's shoulders, each carrying a pitcher of wine, while Wulf and Guido sought out private corners in which to spend the night with their girls. They sang an old Crusaders' marching song, which had originally been very pious but in which, over the years, all the holy images had been replaced by obscene ones. One of the verses, which had once described the Assumption of the Virgin, described instead the carnal relations between the Devil and the Archbiship of Paris, with much detailed description of organs and the orifices to which they were applied.

The two men reeled into the room which held Falcon's gear and half collapsed on the straw-stuffed pallets which lay against the wall. They managed not to spill any wine while doing this.

"So, what are your plans, Draco?" Donal asked, sitting with his back against the plastered wall.

"I seek employment for myself and my men. Would you care to join us? You're the finest ax fighter I've ever known, and I'd like to have you in my following."

"Need you ask? I've been plying my trade by watching warehouses at night. Almost enough to drive a man back to Crusading. Sure, I'll join you. Any prospects yet?"

"Almost," Falcon said. "A lady wished to hire us this very day, but I had to refuse." He told Donal of his interview with the chatelaine of La Roche.

"Ah, Marie de Cleves," Donal said, fingers laced over his paunch. "A handsome lady, as God is my witness. Yes, the story's all over this town. La Roche and Pierre Noir are both less than a day's ride from here." He pondered his twiddling thumbs with drunken intensity. "Actually, I'd been meaning to bring up that feud with you myself, but the evening was so gay I'd determined to put it off till tomorrow."

"Eh? What do you mean?" Falcon asked.

"Did the lady tell you that Thibaut's a cripple?"

"No. What of it?"

"Well, besides being a cripple, he's a coward. He'll not

lead his own men in battle. So he's hired a man to do his leading. A German knight."

"So?" growled Falcon softly. The fumes of the night's excesses were clearing from his head.

"The knight's name is Gunther Valdemar."

Falcon sat, back against the wall, suddenly cold sober. Through his mind went the litany that had been running in it that morning; de Beaumont . . . Edgehill . . . FitzRoy . . . *Valdemar*!

Early the next morning, the lady of La Roche rode out the city gate, followed by Falcon, Wulf, Guido, and Donal. All over the town, and to neighboring communities, word had been passed that the lady's new captain was looking for fighting men.

THREE

MARIE de Cleves was mystified, but dared not question her luck. Early that morning, the strange knight who had saved her from the bear had pounded on her door. He had told her that he'd reconsidered and would take service with her. He'd told her not to worry about pay, that he would see to hiring the men and finding the pay for them.

The man rode at her side now as they took the road for La Roche. Behind them were the Saxon, the Italian, and the ugly Irishmen, along with three of Marie's servingmen. Trying not to seem obvious, she studied the knight beside her. Just now, he wore the anonymity of any other fully armored knight. Except for the extreme fineness of his equipment and the odd Eastern sword, he might have been any feudal fighting man from any part of Europe.

But she remembered how he had looked yesterday, how the terrifying bear that had been about to kill her had collapsed, revealing the huge, handsome man with the white streak in his hair and a wild expression on his face. And what kind of man could kill a bear with a single blow of his fist? Knights had to be strong; they trained from earliest youth in heavy armor, swinging double-heavy weapons for hours every day, year after year.

Still, the feat had been like something out of an old hero tale.

She blushed furiously whenever she thought of her offer to the man yesterday. Would he still hold her to it? Would she really object if he did? Whenever she glanced at him, she felt a growing tingle somewhere deep in her belly, and when she imagined herself lying in bed with him, somehow the guilt her confessor assured her she should feel wouldn't appear.

"My lady," said the knight, breaking in on her thoughts, "how near does this road pass to Thibaut's land?"

"It passes through the village of Deux Eglises, about two miles from here. That village and the land around it belong to Pierre Noir, except for the churches and a monastery called Les Sources."

"Will Thibaut try to stop us when we pass through his land?"

"He may well try, if he has word that we're coming. I saw some of his men at the fair. They may have got word to him by now that I was there, and he knows which way I must come by. Of course, he will expect me to be traveling alone."

"That he will," said Falcon with a wicked smile.

Deux Eglises was a collection of huts made of mud and timber, not dignified by an encircling wall. A ceremony seemed in progress when they arrived, with a procession of monks bearing holy images returning from the fields.

On the road near the procession was a group of a dozen or so horsemen, all but one dressed in armor. The unarmored man was richly dressed, but even from a distance Falcon could tell by the crooked way he sat his horse that the man had a withered leg and a hunched shoulder. The hunchback caught sight of the approaching party and barked something at his men. They wheeled their horses and faced the newcomers, completely blocking the road. Falcon and Marie rode up to him and stopped a few paces away.

"Dearest cousin," said Thibaut, bowing deeply, "well met, indeed. My men and I have just been enjoying the Blessing of the Fields. Would you care to join us?"

"You've never been one to enjoy rustic ceremonies before, cousin," Marie said. "I have affairs that need tending at home. Please let us pass."

Meanwhile, Falcon was hungrily studying the faces of Thibaut's men. He bit back a curse. The one he sought was not there. If he had been, Draco could have settled his business and Marie's with two quick blows of his sword. If a double murder earned him an outlawry in this part of France, well, he had lived with worse.

"Oh, but I must insist, cousin," Thibaut said, and his men began to edge forward. "You must come and be my guest at Pierre Noir. I shall persuade you to consent to my suit and my priest will perform the ceremony this evening."

"I'd sooner marry a leper!" Marie spat.

"Where's Valdemar?" Falcon growled. Thibaut seemed to notice him for the first time.

"Eh? What's that you say, fellow? Valdemar? Who are you?"

"This is my new captain, Sir Draco," Marie said.

"Sir Gunther Valdemar is a great knight and a hero of the Crusade. What does a ragged sell-sword like you want with him?"

"Just a few short words." Falcon said.

"Enough of this," Thibaut said. "Take them. If the armed scum resist, kill them."

"My lords! My lords!" The abbot rushed between the two parties of horsemen, accompanied by a burly young monk who bore a heavy brass crucifix on a long pole. "My lords, this is Saturday—would you violate the Truce of God?" The Truce of God was a church-imposed ban on fighting between Christians between sunset Friday and dawn Monday. To Falcon's knowledge, it had never been seriously observed save when men needed an excuse to rest and rearm. "Please," the abbot continued, "set aside your differences until Monday, and perhaps by that time you will have reached an amicable agreement."

"I've offered her the most amicable agreement of all, abbot. Honorable marriage." He turned to his men. "Take her and kill this rabble."

An overeager knight rushed forward, his horse knocking the abbot to the ground. The young monk swung his crucifix, smashing the man's jaw and hurling him to the road. The sight made Falcon and his men roar with laughter as they spurred their mounts into the midst of Thibaut's men.

In the tight-packed melee there was no room for artistic use of the sword, so Falcon raised his shield and swung his ax, cleaving a shield and removing the arm that held it. Two horsemen closed in on him from either side, and Falcon blocked a blow from the man on his shield side while his horse spun on its forefeet and slammed its iron-plated and spiked hind hooves into the ribs of the horse on the right. Falcon split the skull of the man whose blow he had taken and caught the other in the ribs with a backhand as the injured horse staggered past. Man and horse fought like a single creature with four feet, two hands, and no soul.

With a space now cleared around him, Falcon saw Donal leaning low in his saddle to hew the leg off a rider below his shield. Few men could have accomplished so difficult a blow so easily. He saw the young monk swinging a morningstar he had taken from the man he'd felled. Wulf was on foot as usual, ducking under horses and slitting cinches and stirrup leathers, coming up behind riders to slice at unarmored buttocks as they stood in their in their stirrups to strike, an old Saracen trick familiar to all Crusaders but new here.

Then a horseman in boiled-leather armor was riding at Falcon with his lance lowered. The point was too close to avoid. Most knights would have braced themselves and taken it on the shield, trying to stay in the saddle while the lance shattered. Instead, with his usual uncanny timing, Falcon caught the shaft just behind the head with the upper edge of his shield, lifting it so that the point passed within an inch of his cheek. He stood in his stirrups and brought the ax down where the man's shoulder joined the neck. There was a crunch as the heavy blade smashed through iron-tough leather, through flesh and bone, shearing down through the ribs and at last wedging firmly in the heavy bones of the pelvis. He released the ax as the dead man's horse carried him past, spraying blood like a split wineskin.

Falcon dropped his shield and drew his sword. There was plenty of room to use it now. Things seemed well in hand. A rider was trying to seize Marie, but the man fell with a bolt in his neck, and Falcon saw Guido standing well clear of the brawl, calmly rebracing his bow. Donal rode up to Falcon.

"Still the same, eh, Draco? One blow per man!"

"Who needs more?" Falcon said shrugging his massive mailed shoulders.

"Old Suleiman taught you well, that's a fact. Look at that monk!" Donal pointed to where a final pair of combatants still struggled. The young monk now had a shield, and he was trading blows with one of Thibaut's men who was unhorsed and fighting with shield and longsword. Marie rode up to them.

"Why don't you help that monk? He's not a warrior, and he's aiding us."

"He chose to fight, I didn't command him," Falcon said.

"Besides, my lady," added Donal, "while he's no trained warman, he catches on quickly. If he looks as if he might lose, I'll ax the other bastard, but I'd wager on the monk."

The morningstar the monk had picked up had a two-foot wooden handle, with two feet of chain tipped with a spiked iron ball. Just now, he was landing the ball repeatedly on the other's shield, while blocking the sword with his own shield. This was a waste of the weapon's potential, for the beauty of the morningstar was that its flexibility defeated the defense of the shield. Falcon agreed with Donal, though. The monk had natural talent and would discover the right way to use the weapon soon.

With a wild shout, the swordsman leaped in close, hewing at the monk's knees. The monk lowered his shield to catch the sword and swung a wild overhand blow. The shaft of the morningstar caught the upper edge of the shield and the chain looped over the shield, landing the ball on the man's helmet. The swordsman staggered back, holding the shield high and close. The monk jumped forward and swung horizontally, hitting the shield at waist level. The chain wrapped around the man and slammed the spiked ball into his back over the kidney.

"The monk has it, now," Donal said. The swordsman arched his back and fell, and the monk raised the morningstar for a killing blow, but the abbot seized his arm and restrained him. "There's always a spoilsport," Donal said philosophically.

"You've killed my men!" It was Thibaut, sitting his horse unnoticed well clear of the fight. "You attacked and murdered my men on my own land! You will bear witness to that, abbot!"

"That I will not, my lord!" said the abbot, striding up with the chastened monk in tow. "You set your men upon these people in violation of the Peace of God, and to *that* I will bear witness. You may own this fief, but not the monastery or the churches, and your tame archbishop cannot order me, either. I shall petition the Pope for your excommunication, my lord!"

"Fool! I shall see you and all these others bound before me for my pleasure ere long, and—" His words broke off short as Falcon grasped the front of his clothes and hauled him from his horse. Easily, he held Thibaut dangling several feet above the ground, as he had held the bearkeeper. He drew Thibaut in until his face was inches from Falcon's.

"Pig," Falcon hissed, "the only thing that stays me from carving your crooked carcass right now is that the abbot is too honest to testify that it was not murder. That, and a message I want you to deliver."

"M-message?" stuttered Thibaut, teeth a-chatter. All his bombast was gone and a sour smell rose from him, attesting that in his fear he had fouled himself.

"Tell Gunther Valdemar that Draco Falcon is alive and is here." With his free hand, Falcon tore off his helmet and threw back his coif. "Describe me to him, so he'll know I'm alive in truth. I am easy to remember. Tell him the world is not big enough to hide him and the other three from me. Tell him I won't kill him swiftly, as I kill other men. Tell him you've seen his death, and it's coming for him!" He cast Thibaut into a pile of horse droppings, then rode back to Marie.

"I'm sorry I couldn't kill him for you now, my lady. I don't mind being excommunicated, but you would be held guilty, too."

"There was no help for it. Anyway, I don't want Thibaut killed, richly as he deserves it. I just want to preserve my father's castle and land. What is that mad Irishman doing over there?" She pointed to where Donal was methodically hacking the heads from the corpses and stacking them in a neat pile.

"Oh, that's an old Irish custom that he follows. He's a peculiar man, but a great hand with the ax."

"But those are soldiers, not criminals. Their bodies shouldn't be mutilated," she protested.

"No corpse complains of what happens to it, and Donal tells me that it's honorable treatment in Ireland. Besides, I have it from authority that all will be restored on judgment day." As always, Falcon was amazed that it was considered perfectly all right to torture and kill living men, but that afterward you had to treat their dead bodies with respect.

The area smelled as battlefields always do; of blood and vomit and excrement. The sights and smells became too much for Marie, and she rode into the bushes to be violently ill.

"Donal," Falcon shouted, "when you're done with that chore, fetch my ax from that fellow over there. It may take some carving." Donal waved acknowledgment, and Falcon trotted over to where the abbot was berating the young monk who had fought. His fellow monks, who had been hiding while the fight was in progress, looked at him with distaste mingled with fear.

"Brother Simon," the abbot was saying sadly, "I fear that you have no true vocation to be a monk." Simon hung his head and wore a sheepish expression. "If you have the devil in your soul that makes you take up arms, then perhaps it is best that you take the cross and go to the Holy Land. That way, you may fight and serve God at the same time."

"I have a better suggestion," Falcon said. "I'm hiring soldiers, and you look like good material."

The young monk looked up at him. Falcon was a frightening spectacle with his white blaze of hair and his armor splashed from neck to hem with blood. The monk had a broad face, sandy tonsured hair, and a heavy jaw. He grinned, with the bloody morningstar dangling from a

42

hamlike fist. "I'll join you," he said. "I always wanted to be a soldier. My mother made me join the monastery, to keep me safe, but she's dead now."

"Can you read and write?"

"A little. And I can do sums."

"Good. You're a little old to train with the lance and sword. Will you keep the morningstar?"

The monk hefted the murderous weapon. "It seems to suit me."

"Then when we get to La Roche, turn yourself over to Donal, that maiden-faced Irishman over there collecting heads. He's a master and will train you. See if you can find some armor to fit you." The armor had by now been stripped from the bodies and piled on the road. "I want every man of mine well armed and mounted, so take a horse, too."

Donal came up, wiping off Falcon's ax. "Had a devil of a time getting this out of that fellow's hip. You're getting old, Draco. Time was when you'd cleave a man to the saddle with that blow."

"Saracens are smaller," Falcon said and shrugged.

Marie rode to rejoin them. "For the love of Christ," she said. "Let's ride out of this stench! Is it always like this after a battle?"

"Sometimes it's hotter and smells worse." Falcon said.

Wulf rode up to them and tossed a heavy bag to Falcon. "Careless of you, my lord. I relieved Thibaut of this before he could sneak away. I swear he lamented its loss more than that of his men." Falcon ripped the purse open. It was stuffed with golden ducats.

"What was he going to buy with this?" said Falcon, laughing exultantly.

"Nothing," Marie said. "Thibaut always carries a pouch of gold to run his fingers through at idle moments, the way some men are forever fondling their privates."

43

"This will pay for the hire of a good many men." He tossed the bag up and caught it like a boy with a ball.

"Not enough to match Thibaut's two hundred," Marie reminded him.

"Somewhat less than two hundred now," Falcon said, and his men laughed and punched one another in high good spirits. "And we won't need that many, in any case, if most of Thibaut's men are like that lot. I've an idea for how to raise a force, something I've been turning over in my head since I left the Holy Land."

When they reached the small village and castle of La Roche, they saw to their horses and cleaned their weapons and armor, then all filed into the dim, smoky great hall for supper.

La Roche was an old-fashioned castle, with a central stone keep surrounded by a man-made earthen rampart topped by a wall of sharpened logs. Falcon's expert eye studied it inside and out. After the giant fortifications of Palestine and Syria, it seemed small and shabby. Worse, it was obsolete. Men with siege experience in the Holy Land could take such a place in an afternoon. It was good enough a generation ago, when warfare was mostly neighborly feuding, but it could not stand against a master of siegecraft like Valdemar.

When supper was over and the trenchers cleared away, Falcon spoke of his plans.

"Thibaut has some two hundred men. Most of them will be poorly armed rabble, good only for running down wounded men and burning peasants' huts. Word has gone out that I am hiring men, but I won't be satisfied with that sort of trash. We have here some master fighters. Guido with his crossbow, Donal with the axe, Wulf with the falchion and buckler, and Simon bids fair to become a champion with the morningstar. Any of us is worth a pack of untrained villeins. I will hire on that basis, taking only men who are masters with their weapons, or who can be trained. Fifty should be sufficient to start with." All the others nodded at the wisdom of this.

"That is the first part of my plan. Here is the second. Before the Crusade, men served their lord in return for land and protection. They could give only forty days' service under arms because they had to care for their land the rest of the time. In recent years, the Crusade has brought forth the hired soldier, who works for wages and can trade one master for another. Most work as individual sell-swords. I propose building an army of such men." His followers wore looks of intense concentration, striving to follow his new ideas. They were little used to thinking, and new ideas were always things to be regarded with suspicion.

"The best thing about such a force," Falcon went on, "is that it can serve as long as there's pay. In fact, it can fight all year round."

"But who can fight in winter?" Marie asked. "There's no grass for the horses then. Hereabouts, the hosting is always held in early June, when the grass is high enough to feed the horses."

"In winter, we'll have to fight on foot."

"On foot!" exclaimed Marie. "My father and others like him would never fight dismounted, except at a siege. Where will you find men of knightly rank who will consent to fight in the field dismounted?"

"Returning Crusaders," Falson said. "In the Holy Land, everyone has to learn to fight afoot sooner or later, because the horses die of sickness even faster than the men. The Saracen breed are swift, but too small to bear a Frankish knight and his armor." Saracens called all Europeans Franks, no matter what their nation.

"When we've settled this matter of Thibaut," Falcon continued, "we'll stay together, instead of going our separate ways, as hired soldiers usually do."

"But," Marie said, alarmed, "I cannot support fifty

men all through the winter! How will I feed and pay them?"

"Have no fear, my lady," Falcon said, patting her hand and sending a tingle all the way to her shoulder. "The best thing of all about the force I propose is that it can pick up its gear and leave at any time. When this fight is over, we'll just go and look for another fight."

"But," said Simon, the ex-monk, "what if there's no fight to take up?" The others roared with laughter at such a thought.

"Then," Donal said, tears streaming down his face, "start saying your prayers, lad, because that'll signify that the Lord Jesus has come back and the end of the world is at hand!" Simon flushed and lapsed into silence.

Marie de Cleves sat brushing her hair in her shift as she sat before the tall, polished sheet of bronze that served for a looking glass. She had lit several candles and their light flooded the chamber with a buttery glow. At least the stripping of the castle had given her a privacy unknown to earlier generations. It was an age when even the nobility slept in crowded rooms, as often as not four or five to a bed. Her tresses, freed from their wimple, were wavy and chestnut-colored.

She contemplated Draco Falcon. Such a hard, savage man, yet with so many facets and shadings. Hacking a man nearly in two at one moment, at another enraged that someone had tortured a bear. And the way he looked at her, as if he saw through clothes to the flesh beneath, and through the flesh to the soul. Sometimes, when she was near him, her lips felt somehow swollen, and her breasts heavy. He made her conscious of her body in a way she had not experienced in a very long time.

She was not a virgin. When she was fifteen, there had been a clerk in her father's service who had been only a little older than she. He had played the lute for her, and sung the love songs of the trouvères. They had fallen in love, and in the flower-laden fields had explored one another. By great good fortune, she had not been gotten with child, and before she had really discovered the possibilities in her ripening young body, he had followed her father to Palestine. In time, word had come back that he had died of a pestilence. She had mourned, but everybody was mourning a great deal in those years. It had passed, but sometimes she still dreamed of him, and awoke with an ache in her loins that she had to assuage in the only way she could.

On an impulse, she stood. Her hand went to the knot at the shoulder of her shift and pulled it free. The cloth slid down to pool at her feet, and she examined herself in the mirror as she had in those years when her body had been changing from the angles of girlhood to the curves of a woman.

Her skin was very white, though the bronze mirror transformed it alchemically to gold. Her breasts were large and shapely, with generous brown nipples surrounded by broad aureolae. She was twenty-two, and as yet they had no trace of sag. Hesitantly, she ran her hands over them, cupping their fullness and imagining that the hands were his. The tingle shot all the way down to her gently mounded belly, and centered someplace behind the rich nest of dark curls that covered her lower belly and the plump mound at the joining of her legs.

Her waist was narrow, flaring into sleek hips and long, tapering thighs. Her calves were slim and her ankles shapely. She turned and looked back over her shoulder. Her back tapered smoothly to the waist, then spread into the full roundness of her buttocks, each surmounted by a deep round identation. She was satisfied. When the time came, he would find her beautiful.

But how many women must he have known in his travels? It was said that the Saracen women were trained from birth in all the ways to please a man, that their skins were plucked clean of every hair, and rubbed with pumice stones daily, and massaged with scented oils to make them smooth and soft and fragrant. What would she seem like to him? Probably he would think her a clumsy French country girl who smelled like a woman and nothing else, who had hair between her legs and under her arms and knew only how to lie back and spread her legs and welcome her lover with joy but no cunning.

Well, he would just have to teach her, and he would find her a willing pupil. Without redonning her shift, she snuffed the candles and slid beneath the comforters of her bed. She lay on her side and drew up her knees. Almost, her hand strayed between her thighs. No. Even if it meant losing some sleep, she would wait.

FOUR

WULF surveyed the crowd of men in the bailey—the open, grassy field between the encircling timber palisade and the stone keep. He sat on the corner of a trestle table set up in the yard while Simon sat on a bench with parchment, quills, and ink before him, ready to take down the names of the men chosen for service.

"My Lord Draco Falcon," Wulf shouted, "is hiring men for his company. He is now in the service of Lady Marie de Cleves, but those chosen here will take service with him alone, to go at his bidding wherever it pleases him. Those among you who only wish to defend La Roche against Thibaut and his German butcher, go to the other side of the bailey, where Donal MacFergus will assign you places to defend, and arms to bear, should it come to a siege."

Perhaps half the men crossed the bailey to where the Irishman stood beside a pile of spears and clubs. The rest were mostly armed and armored, obviously professionals. They had been gathering for several days, as word had spread about the hiring at La Roche.

Many of them came mounted and fully armored, knights or sergeants who were of less than knightly rank but had learned the art of horseback fighting in the wars.

The Crusades had brought about much blurring of social distinctions.

"My lord wants only the best; no lackeys and none who only run in to kill the wounded. Every man must know his weapons and every man must fight as fiercely as the bravest. My lord misses nothing on the battlefield or in the camp. Those who shirk their duties will be expelled from the company without pay and with their arms and mounts confiscated. Those who are seen to be cowards in battle he will hang.

"Every man—knight, sergeant, and footman—will bear a hand in tending castle and camp, and in standing sentry duty. We will tow with us no rabble to shovel shit, cook, and clean. Any who are too proud to soldier in such a fashion may leave now." At this, three or four well-dressed knights wheeled their horses and rode away with disappointed scowls.

"There go some carpet-knights," Wulf muttered to Simon. "No man who's campaigned in Palestine objects to sentry-go and hauling shit."

The horsemen were tested first. Wulf hung a cinch ring, about three inches in diameter, from a gibbet. As each horseman lowered his lance, he set the ring swinging. Any man who could not spear the ring five times out of five was rejected. For the final test, Falcon himself led those who could perform the ring-spearing out to a small spring near the castle. Each man was made to jump his horse over the stream. When all four of the horse's feet were in the air, the man had to lean out of his saddle and slice the water cleanly, without raising a spray, and land on the other side with his mount under perfect control. Of more than fifty horsemen tested, only fifteen passed.

Next came the foot soldiers' turn. Each man had to fight in turn against Wulf, Donal, and Falcon with his chosen weapon, whether it be ax, sword, spear, glaive, mace, morningstar, or other. He also had to show proficiency with the weapons which were not his own first choice, and all had to be expert with the dagger.

When the hand-to-hand testing was done, Wulf called for missile troops. Slingers and javelin throwers were rejected, as these weapons were now regarded as obsolete. He accepted one man who was a master of the vanishing art of the throwing ax. There were three crossbowmen, all Genoese like Guido, for that city had excelled in the weapon for centuries, and had a near monopoly on its experts.

Wulf had a few slots left when he looked up from the table to see two tall men, brothers from the look of them. Both were brown-haired and green-eyed, and they wore no armor, not so much as a steel cap. Their only sidearms were long knives at their belts, but they carried the biggest bows Wulf had ever seen. "Names?" he asked.

"Gower and Rhys ap Gwynneth," said one. Simon struggled with a Latin spelling for the names.

"You two may as well leave," Wulf said. "Stick bows like those are no good anymore. They won't penetrate mail."

Falcon came from where he had been observing the horsemen to check on Wulf's progress. One of the bowmen pointed to the door of the keep, some fifty paces away. "Watch," he said. Phlegmatically, he set the lower end of his bow against his left instep and pushed the upper loop of the bowstring into its retaining notch. Selecting a yard-long, pile-headed arrow from his quiver, he nocked it, raised the bow, and drew. Unlike the flat, sharp-edged hunting point, the pile head was small, solid, and triangular or square in cross-section for penetrating mail. Wulf noted that he drew on the string with three fingers instead of two, and that he drew to the ear, like a Saracen, instead of to the chest as the common European short bow was drawn. He released smoothly and the arrow thunked into the door.

"So you can hit a door at fifty paces," Wulf shrugged. "You'll have to do better than that to be taken on here."

"Go look at it," the archer said. He spoke with an outlandish accent so thick that he was not easy to understand.

Suspiciously, Wulf went to the door. He grasped the arrow and tried to draw it out. It wouldn't budge. Falcon came up and opened the door. The arrowhead protruded through the other side of the five-inch oaken door. The two men looked at each other and returned to where the archer stood. Falcon held out his hand and was handed the bow. He examined it. At the center, it was as thick as a man's two thumbs held together, and it tapered evenly to the limbs. It was crude and rough-looking, as if whittled by a child and not finished. It was apparently made of yew or ash or elm. He handed it to Wulf. The Saxon drew it, struggling to get it to full draw.

"Christ, it's stiffer than your Saracen bow!"

"Where are you two from?" Falcon demanded.

"Cymru," said the archer who had not yet spoken.

"What's that?" asked Simon.

"Wales," Wulf said. "It's a country to the west of England."

"I've heard them talking together in their own tongue," Simon said, remembering the strange, musical language that was full of sibilants and liquid vowel sounds. "I took them for Bretons."

"The tongues are almost the same," said the archer who had shot. He said some words to his brother in the odd tongue and pointed to a crow that was circling high above the keep. The other man strung his own bow, nocked a shaft, then aimed and fired all in one smooth motion. The bird's flight intersected the arrow's arc and it fell to the ground. There were low whistles at the feat.

"How high would you judge it, my lord?" Wulf asked.

"Ten seconds of a hawk's climb—say, two hundred

paces." He turned to Simon. "Hire them." The ex-monk scratched his head.

"How shall I write 'Wales'? Latin has no letter for the first sound." He tried "Ualis," then scratched it out.

"Write it as 'Cambria.' That's what the Romans called it." Falcon took the quill from Simon's hand and wrote the word himself. Simon and all the other men except Wulf stared in open-mouthed amazement. A knight who could read and write was an unheard-of prodigy. They would have been further amazed to know that besides French and Latin, he could write Greek, Arabic, and even a little Hebrew.

Their last hiring of the day was a special bonus. He was an unlikely prize, for he was a potbellied, gray-bearded man with one eye. He was known as Rupert Foul-Mouth, for his skill at vituperation and blasphemy earned him the stunned admiration of even the most seasoned campaigners. He had been a woodworker by trade in his youth, and was now a master builder of catapults and other siege engines, of shelters and mantlets, and could even throw up a temporary castle within days wherever there was timber. He was also adept at tunneling and sapping enemy fortifications and at demolishing walls. A man of his skill was worth many fighting men, and he knew it and demanded higher pay than the others. Falcon agreed without haggling.

"I'm pleased as the Devil's cock in a bishop's bunghole to be your man, sir," said Rupert, "and you'll for fucked sure never regret employing me ale-soaked shitten old carcass in your bleeding service."

When the choosing was over, Falcon lined up the men for inspection. He made double sure that all had good eyes and sound teeth and all their fingers, and he examined all their feet to make sure they could stand long marches. Even the horsemen were subjected to this humiliation.

When he was fully satisfied, he made a last progress down the line. One after another, each man knelt, placed his folded hands between Falcon's, and took the same oath he had given Guido. When the ceremony was over, he handed the best horseman his new banner, which Marie and her ladies had cut and embroidered for him. Like his shield, it depicted the black falcon clutching the bolts of blue lightning against a silver field. Simon came to him and gave him the final list he had drawn up of the company's personnel, with their names, places of origin, rates of pay, and specialties.

"Many are called, but few are chosen," Simon said.

It was a foggy morning, and that was all to the good. The horse herd occupied a wide meadow near a small village. Six armed men guarded the horses, and there were a dozen or so unarmed varlets to tend them. Several of the thirty or more horses were destriers—stallions trained to war that had to be picketed separately lest they fight one another. The rest were common riding and hunting beasts.

Falcon and his cavalrymen had ridden in the night to the edge of the forest on a rise of ground overlooking the meadow, their horses' hoofs wrapped in straw to muffle them. Just now, the straw wrappings were being removed. They were no longer necessary.

Falcon had determined that all of his men should be trained to ride at least well enough to be able to keep up with the horsemen. Mobility was important to a small force, and he didn't want the kind of army that draggled along at the pace of the slowest walker. The problem was finding the horses. The solution was simple. Thibaut would supply them, as he had supplied the money for the troop's first payday.

At a signal from Falcon, they rode out, hallooing and yipping, encircling the herd. The armed men looked up in shock, then scrambled for their weapons and mounts. They had no time to brace themselves for battle before Falcon's men were upon them. They milled about uncertainly, outnumbered and at sword's point.

"Yield if you would live," Falcon said. One by one, the men dropped their weapons and dismounted, heads hanging. They were efficiently stripped of armor and their horses taken to join the herd, which was now being driven toward La Roche.

"You men," Falcon said, "may now go. Spread the word that those who yield to me will be spared. Those who resist will be killed." One of the peasant herdsmen came up to Falcon, his cap twisted in his hands.

"Will you be burning the village now, sir?" he asked.

"Eh? What's that?" Falcon asked.

"I asked if you'd be burning the village, sir. The knights usually do when Lord Thibaut loses a fight hereabouts. We'd be most grateful if you'd let us keep some food for winter and not molest our womenfolk."

"I make war on soldiers, not on peasants," Falcon said, and the man looked at him in amazement. "Your village is safe, man. Go home." Sometimes it was necessary to devastate a countryside in order to deny food and shelter to a foe, but Falcon had always been disgusted with the kind of stupid, wanton, childlike destruction most soldiers delighted in. He'd known armies to starve through winter because they had destroyed villages and crops for the sheer joy of it.

Not, of course, that his gesture would do much good. Thibaut would probably burn the village and hang all the men for losing the horses, anyway. The thought did not distress him greatly. If men would not fight for what was theirs, they deserved to lose all they had. He had long ago divided all of mankind into two camps: those who would fight, and those who would not. He knew which camp always prevailed.

Back at La Roche, he began drilling the men mercilessly. Those who could not ride had to learn. Those used to fighting as individuals had to learn teamwork. The bowmen had to learn to coordinate and concentrate their work. They had been accustomed to picking off the most convenient targets. Now they had to learn to give the best support they could to the other arms. All had to learn to organize quickly into work gangs under Rupert's foulmouthed direction. Falcon hoped one day to have an army divided into separate arms that could operate independently or together. He especially wanted a siege train of skilled engineers, carpenters, miners, and sappers, but that was many years down the road. For now, every man had to learn to be a jack-of-all-trades.

A few of the men were already skilled in this new type of warfare; men who had been to the Crusades. That endless series of campaigns was gradually forging the armed rabble of Europe into a disciplined army under the painful tutelage of a fierce, brilliant, and civilized enemy.

Draco Falcon had spent half his life in the wars in the huge area of Syria, Palestine, and Egypt that the Europeans referred to simply as Outremer—"Oversea." As he sat his horse, his eyes clouded over, and Wulf knew that he was no longer seeing the men drilling before him. He was once more standing on the sands of Outremer. He was living in his memories of the war, and of Valdemar.

Draco de Montfalcon, nineteen years old, was on the run. The bloody ruin of the Horns of Hattin was two days past. He had been fighting under the banner of Raymond of Tripoli that day, or he would have been slaughtered with the rest. Instead, he had escaped, only to find himself separated from the little band of escapees in the confusion of the nighttime flight. Alone of the few survivors, he knew of the betrayal that had caused the catastrophic battle.

In future months, when word of the calamity reached Europe, Christendom would be rocked. The news was staggering; a Christian army of thirty thousand annihilated; Guy of Lusignan, King of Jerusalem, a prisoner; Reginald de Chatillon personally beheaded by Saladin himself; all the captured Templars and Hospitalers executed. Perhaps worst of all, the True Cross had been captured. Ominously, after nearly a hundred years of the Crusades, the Saracens were at last beginning to behave with the savagery that the Christians had always displayed. All over Christendom, churchmen were straining themselves to explain how God could have allowed such a thing to happen. Some tortured theology would follow in years to come.

Just now, Draco had no thoughts for the battle or events at home. He was concerned for his life and that of his companion, the Saxon horse boy Wulf. The boy was fourteen and very frightened. A livid ring of scar tissue around his throat showed where he had worn an English thrall ring for many years. He had followed the armies since stowing away on a Crusader ship at Devon five years before. For the last two, he had been caring for Draco's horse, and the two young men had become close friends—a thing forbidden by social custom in Europe but common enough in the freewheeling society of Outremer and the Crusader camps, where whores sat at the tables of kings and varlets could become knights, did they but prove themselves. In a world where knights could actually wield bows from horseback, anything was possible.

"I'll get them, Wulf," Draco was saying, still a bit dazed from the clout he'd taken on the head at Hattin. He'd stripped off armor and helm in the flight, and had finally cast away his shield and kept only his sword; a long, broad, two-edged blade that he'd finally grown big enough to wield. "I'll get the four of them, Gunther Valdemar and Archbishop de Beaumont and Nigel Edgehill, but most of all, if I must consecrate my entire life to it, I'll get Odo FitzRoy, and then . . ." There followed a long list of ingenious and obscene tortures which Wulf had been hearing unceasingly for days.

"Yes, my lord, we'll do that, that we shall. Now you just get back here behind the rocks and hide with me. It's almost dark and we can set out then. We've got to get to the coast and get away, then we'll see about Odo Fitzroy and the others." He talked soothingly, as one talks to a child or when humoring a madman. Draco had always been a little strange, almost daft, and the events of recent weeks, first his father, then the catastrophe at Hattin, had driven him to the very edge of sanity. Men said that the lightning had been the cause of his earlier strangeness. Wulf had heard talk by some of the men who had survived the fight off Cyprus along with Eudes and Draco. Draco, a half-grown boy, had regained consciousness a day after being struck by the bolt, the only one so struck to have survived, although badly scarred and burned. He'd been in a raving delirium for days, then had come out of it.

He was changed, though. He was now subject to wild fits of rage and deep depressions followed by days of uproarious mirth. One day he might strike down any man near him, the next day he would dance and sing all day and night without pause to eat or sleep. There had been another effect, too. He was still a boy, too small to use a man's full-sized weapons, but in his mad rages he seemed to gain the strength of two men. Wulf had seen four knights hard pressed to restrain Draco in one of his demonic bouts. Among the superstitious soldiers it was beginning to be said that he had somehow absorbed the strength of the lightning when it could not kill him. Eudes protested that his son was merely a little addled from the experience, and that it would pass in time. Still, the strange yough was regarded with awe within the army.

They were nearing the coast when the Saracens caught them. They had been without water for two days, and the sight of the clump of palms meant a spring. Had they been older and more experienced, they would have shown more caution, lying low and watching the oasis all night and all the next day if need be before entering it. But they lacked the ingrained self-discipline of seasoned campaigners.

Draco was at the edge of the trees when the noose fell over his shoulders, pinning his arms tight. With a growl, he exerted his great strength to break it, but the braided horsehair rope defeated his efforts. In seconds, more ropes were pinioning his wrists and ankles. He saw that Wulf was in the same predicament, and he felt a sharp stab of shame. Wulf was his follower, and he had led the boy into a trap. His father would have been unforgiving of such a lapse.

Laughing voices speaking the Saracen tongue came from the trees. Robed and turbaned figures became faintly visible in the dim light preceding the dawn. Then, unbelievably, he heard a voice speaking the rough French patois of the Crusader kingdoms!

"So, more stragglers from the battle, eh?" A hulking figure in Saracen clothes came to where Draco was lying helplessly and nudged him hard in the ribs with his toe. "A fine pair of strappling lads, too. They'll fetch a good price from some galley captain." Draco didn't need the growing light to know who was speaking. The heavy German accent and guttural voice were enough without needing to see the drooping yellow walrus mustache or the fat, upturned pig nose. It was Valdemar, one of the men he'd sworn to kill, and he was at the swine's mercy. Draco ground his face into the sand in rage and frustration.

"Well, if it isn't young Draco, son of my old friend Eudes." He broke into uproarious laughter. "You should

59

have known every water hole for miles around the battle site would be watched for stragglers. Eudes would never have been so foolish." Draco's humiliation was unbearable, for the man's words were true. "Well, I should have known that the boy the lightning couldn't kill would survive that little skirmish at Hattin."

"You betrayed the True Cross and gave it to the Saracens!" Draco shouted. "You let the greatest army of Christendom be wiped out! And my father—" Valdemar kicked him in the mouth.

"Silence, whelp. Ah, yes, the True Cross or Holy Rood or what you will; and then, there's the Sacred Lance, which pierced the Savior's side. Haven't you learned yet, boy, that those things are just tricks to keep men fighting when it makes more sense to quit? One of my Saracen friends has a hair from the beard of the Prophet that he swears by and says it gives his arm strength in battle. It probably came off the arse of a goat, but if it helps him, where's the harm? Just don't ask me to believe it. I give no loyalty to man or God, my lad. I've sold my loyalty elsewhere." Despite his predicament, Draco's mind whirled at the implications. Had the man sold his soul to Satan for success on earth? And if he had, what of the others? What chance had he against the might of the Prince of Darkness?

For three days, chained neck to neck with Wulf and a dozen other wretches, Draco marched across the scorching July sands to the coast. Valdemar spoke no more to him until he was sold with Wulf and some others to a galley master. He was numb with despair. It was known that the living death of a galley, whether Christian or heathen, was the very closest thing to the agonies of hell that could be contrived by man. He was stripped naked and chained to a bench behind an oar that he and Wulf would pull together for the next two years. Only his lust for revenge kept him from contemplating suicide.

Before he left, Valdemar came to the bench for a few final words with Draco.

"I'm happy to report that I got a decent price for you two." He tossed up a pouch of coins and caught it again. "I've told the master that you seem to be unkillable, so he need not spare the whip. Actually, I'm pleased that you are so difficult to slay. It means that you'll spend a good many years on this pleasant boat before wearing out. No man is immune to the ravages of time, after all." He pointed to a huge, grossly fat, shaven-headed man in a loincloth. He had a black, drooping mustache and a face full of jagged scars. He wore broad leather bracelets and carried a long braided black whip that coiled in his massive paw like a serpent. "His name is Abu and he's the overseer. He's been kicked off a dozen galleys for his cruelty, and I will leave to your imagination what that implies. He has a fondness for hashish and for handsome lads like you and your Saxon friend here. When he bends you over the rail, I suggest you relax; it hurts much less that way. Who knows? You may acquire a taste for it. You might as well, because you'll be enduring it for a long, long time." He slapped his thigh and laughed uproariously again, then strode up the gangplank to the dock.

With dread, Draco saw Abu coming toward their bench, wearing on his ugly face a savage leer.

FIVE

THIBAUT de Cleves was agitated and nervous. Across from him sat the German knight he'd thought fearless. For the last year, Valdemar had been managing Thibaut's forces with an efficient savagery that matched Thibaut's greed. They made a good pair, and had been gobbling up the smaller nearby fiefs while their masters were away Crusading, the crime abbetted by the local archbishop, who was firmly in Thibaut's purse and protected him from the terrible sentence of excommunication.

In all that time, even in the direst extremity of battle, Thibault had never seen the German show the slightest trace of fear. The man was an expressionless, emotionless fighting machine and he inflicted the most hideous tortures with the same calm demeanor that he brought to counting his loot.

But he had gone pale beneath his Crusader's tan when Thibaut had told him of Falcon, and had described to him the white streak and the white line down his face.

"Draco!" he had half whispered. "The name's a bit different, but it must be he! Couldn't be otherwise, if you saw the marks on his face. How could he have survived the galley and escaped? Lord Satan, but what a warrior he must be by now!" The German fell to pulling at his mustache while Thibaut quivered with dread at his oath. Valdemar never attended Mass or took communion, and Thibaut was careful not to inquire about the rites he performed behind the barred door of his chamber, but now he feared that his worst suspicions had been far short of the mark.

"With a Saracen sword, you say? That's something he must have learned since I knew him. Was there a yellow-haired Saxon with him? About twenty-four or five?"

"How should I know?" Thibaut said testily. "Am I supposed to take note of every base varlet my cousin employs?" Valdemar had turned and stalked away, leaving Thibaut mystified.

Now it was two weeks later and Valdemar was in full possession of himself, and even seemed to take a certain sardonic amusement in the turn of events. Thibaut was not sure which attitude frightened him more.

"What has passed between you and this Falcon?" Thibaut asked.

"He's a man I knew in Outremer. Little more than a boy, then, really. I had him in my power once and I should have killed him then, but I allowed myself to inflict something worse on him instead. I suppose mercy really does have its place, after all. Well, a man is what he's made himself, so I shall not complain." The German's strange, pessimistic philosophy sent chills into Thibaut. Had the man no concern for salvation? Every night, Thibaut agonized over the fate of his own soul, and every day his greed and lust drove him to ever greater sins.

"What did this man do to offend you so?" Thibaut asked.

"Nothing. His father was my friend."

"Eh?" Thibaut said, puzzled. This was just what he needed; a mortal feud between two mad Crusaders that had nothing to do with his lust for his cousin and her land, but that might well destroy both fiefs.

63

"Forget that," Valdemar said. "It doesn't concern you. What does is that some of your cousin's men stole a herd of your horses this morning."

"What? Which herd?"

"The one at Tres Routes."

"Tres Routes?" Thibaut tore at his hair. "More than thirty of my best stock taken! Who allowed this to happen? Hang the soldiers and burn the village! I want all the villagers flogged. No, I want them hanged. Thirty horses!" He buried his head in his arms, on the point of tears.

"Calm yourself, Thibaut," Valdemar said. He poured a cup of wine for his employer and one for himself. "The soldiers took to their heels, of course. An easy thing to do, since they'd been lightened by the weight of their weapons and armor. They're long gone, now. As for the village, it's valuable property, so why destroy it?"

"Well, yes, I suppose you're right, but I must punish *somebody*!" Thibaut soothed the pain of his lost horses with a long pull at the wine.

"Why not Draco?" Valdemar said. "And what about your haughty cousin? You want to bed her so badly that you've stopped hauling the kitchen girls up to your chamber. Surely seeing her pretty flesh under your whip should be some satisfaction?"

"Yes, of course, but that must be private. She's highborn, after all, and we can't let everybody see her humiliation." Thibaut began to drool at the pictures Valdemar's words put into his mind. "There must be a public example to show my people that they can't allow my property to be stolen with impunity."

"Very well," Valdemar said. "I'll go over to Tres Routes and hang the headman and a dozen or so others." He stood and took his helmet up from the table and shoved it beneath his mailed arm. "Meanwhile, you had better think on why Draco stole those horses."

"Why, he stole . . . well, to sell them and hire more men, I suppose. I'm told he only hired fifty."

"And with your money. Think about this. Suppose he proposes to mount the entire force?"

"Put archers and spearmen on horseback?" exclaimed Thibaut, flabbergasted. "It's unthinkable! How could a wellborn knight commit such a sin against his own class?"

Valdemar shoved his face close to Thibaut's, so that the winy breath washed over him with every word. "A real warrior, you ninny! The kind of soldier that I've seen campaigning in Outremer for the last twenty years. He got the pretty songs and the hero stories knocked out of him long ago and all he cares about now is winning wars, not what the troubadors will sing about him after he's dead. Get used to it, for you'll be seeing a lot more like him in the years to come." He jammed his helmet on his head over the iron-studded leather coif. "Like me, too, for that matter." He whirled on his heel and stalked away in a rustle of mail links clicking together. Thibaut shuddered. What had the times produced?

"Strike!" The man swung his heavy sword at Falcon. Falcon leaned far forward and stepped in under the ponderously descending arm. He came up behind the man and slipped an arm around his chest, lifting him off the ground and presenting a dagger point at the exposed throat with the other hand. He released the swordsman. "That's how it's done," he said to the men seated in a circle around the combatants. The dagger lesson had been going on all morning. Even experts like the two Welshmen were required to attend.

"With the dagger, you must get close," he went on. The points he was making were obvious ones, but most of these men had absorbed daggerplay as boys and had never thought about the theory. Some of them had bad habits to unlearn, and in any case, Falcon wanted every

65

one of them to understand the craft the way he understood the sword or the archers their skills. "There's no sense stabbing or cutting at mail. A swinging arm is hard to hit, and you expose yourself by bending low to slash at a leg, so your targets are the face and throat. Of these, your best bet is the throat. If you attack from in front, your man can protect his throat by simply lowering his chin and hunching his shoulders. No man can defend his throat from behind. Go straight in just below the ear and then straight out. He'll die as he falls. Next!"

All through the long day, he took them through weapons drill. He required that armor always be worn during training, to keep the men accustomed to the weight. He also made sure that they keep all their iron clean and polished and all their leather oiled. It was unbelievable to men accustomed to the slovenly camps and forts of Europe, but they obeyed. They began to take pride in their turnout, and Falcon noted that they had taken to laundering and patching their clothing more frequently, though he had not required this.

Falcon looked up and saw a figure watching from the castle battlement. It was Marie. The sun was lowering and it was time to dismiss the men. Wearily, he walked to the keep and climbed the stair to the battlement. He found Marie alone, a rarity in the now-crowded castle. She smiled when she saw him come through the turret door onto the wallwalk.

"I'm glad you've come to join me, Falcon. I was admiring your band. I've never seen such a change in men in so short a time. They looked like a pack of villainous cutthroats when they arrived. Now they've come to look and act a little like you."

"Pride's not something you're born with, no matter what the stories say. Nor is honor. Men have to earn both."

"That isn't what I was raised to believe," Marie said

uncomfortably. It always bothered her when Falcon talked like this, as if birth and breeding were of little account. He stood with his hand resting on the hilt of his greatsword, head erect as always.

"You've never told me about this sword," she said, her hand reaching out to touch the crescent pommel. "It seems to mean much to you, yet there is no place for saints' relics on it, and no prayers inscribed."

"Not likely," Falcon said with a laugh. "It was the gift of a man called Suleiman the Wise."

"Suleiman? A Saracen gave you this?"

"He was the finest man I ever knew, except for my father. I sometimes think of him as my second father." Marie was horrified at these words but said nothing. Falcon seldom spoke of his past, and she wanted to hear more. "The sword was named Three Moons, for the three curves of the hilt, pommel, and blade. It's a famous sword in the East, said to have been carried by a giant in the days of Harun al-Rashid. When he was satisfied that I merited it, Suleiman belted it to my waist with his own hands."

"So that you could continue Crusading and killing heathens with it?" Marie said.

"I've killed as many Christians, if not more. What else is a knight's trade? It's all the same." More disturbing words. But it was true that most of the knights she had known were common butchers who would as soon kill and rob their fellow Christians as fight the heathen.

"At first," Falcon went on, "Suleiman was my captor. Then he became my teacher. Finally, he became like a father."

"Did you serve him? As a knight, I mean?"

"I did. I would have served him as a wine-pourer, though, once I had come to know him. Though of course he didn't drink wine."

"Did you serve him . . . against Christians?" It made her a little sick to ask, but she had to know.

"Yes," he answered. He looked at her levelly. "It happens far more often than you might think, in Outremer and in Spain. Christian allies with Moslem against Christian. The Saracens do the same, allying with us against their own folk. When it's a question of defending or taking land, religion takes second place."

"Sir Draco," she said, visibly upset, "I had thought you a good knight, though a hard one. Now I don't know what to think. Your words border on blasphemy."

"Don't tell me of blasphemy!" said Falcon angrily. "I've seen more blasphemy committed in the name of Christ or honor than will ever haunt your dreams, lady. Be thankful that your experiences of war and knightly behavior have been confined to songs and petty affrays like that on the road when we came here. Imagine that little bloodletting magnified a thousandfold. Imagine yourself kneeling in prayer in a Christian church with blood flowing around your knees. I've seen that, and far worse." Marie was too stunned by his vehemence to speak.

"You asked about the sword. When my father and Suleiman, the only two men I ever really loved and respected, were dead, I renamed this sword. I decided to return to Christendom, to win my fortune and gain my revenge with it. To live by the sword as all knights do and few will admit. Other men give their swords braggart names, or saints' names, or the names of swords from the old poems, like Durendal or Joyeuse or Excalibur. But I named mine Nemesis."

"Nemesis?" Marie said, puzzled. The name meant nothing to her. "What does that mean?"

"It's something I learned in my studies with Suleiman and old Abraham. Among the old Greeks, before even the days of the Romans, Nemesis was the goddess of vengeance. It seemed a fitting name. I've dedicated my life to the killing of four men. One of them now commands Thibaut's troops at Pierre Noir. She must kill those four before she can have back her old name of Three Moons."

"A heathen name to replace a Saracen one," Marie said. "I think your conception of knighthood differs from my father's. He always said that he could judge the quality of a knight by how he revered his sword—what he named it and the respect in which he held it. His own sword was named Guardian, and when he was not wearing it it was kept on the altar of the castle chapel. It had relics of St. Denis in the pommel, and Father believed it invincible in battle, as long as his cause was just."

"It didn't keep him out of a Turkish prison," Falcon said brutally. "Nemesis may be the finest sword in the world, but it's no magic blade. It's a piece of sharp steel made to kill, and it will keep food in my belly and a horse under my saddle and a roof over my head when I need it. It will protect my life and the lives of those I value, and what I take I will defend with it!" His voice had risen almost to a shout, and Marie shrank against the battlement, frightened by his wild expression. Then one of his lightning changes of mood came over him and the ferocious glare was replaced by a smile.

"It must be nearly time for dinner, my lady," he said. He held forth his hand. "May I escort you to the hall?" Shakily, she took his hand. In the narrow, winding stairway she was acutely conscious of his nearness, of his intensely masculine scents of iron and leather and sweat. It made her knees tremble.

Dinner had been a merry affair. All the men were feeling very full of themselves, what with their success in the horse raid and their new pride in serving under the Falcon banner. More than that, their new allegiance went beyond a mere change of paymaster. They were being transformed into something they had not been before, something there was as yet no name for; a band of men united by a common occupation, a common banner, and something which would one day be called unit pride.

The food had been lavish. With so many nobles absent overseas, taking their huntsmen with them, game abounded in the forests. These days, even the peasants, who in most years lived on nothing but barley porridge, could go out at night and poach meat for the family. It was a hanging offense, but the courts were too understaffed to take notice. Falcon's Genoese crossbowmen had been practicing in the forest, and the two Welshmen had made a foray onto Thibaut's land and brought back many deer and plump fowl. It pleased Falcon that Thibaut was feeding his men, as well as paying and mounting them.

Marie quickly got over her shock at Falcon's disturbing words on the wallwalk. A horseman of Falcon's named Gaston du Vexin and some companions had waylaid a wagonload of splendid wine on its way to Pierre Noir and brought it to La Roche. Falcon had rewarded them with one of the wine casks, to drink or sell as they saw fit. The wine helped in soothing the impact of Falcon's unorthodox philosophy. When she thought about it deeply, she realized that he had articulated many things she had nursed in her mind for many years but had never dared to voice. How was one killing murder, and another an act of religion? If all were descended from Adam and Eve, why were some lords and others peasants?

Falcon was seated at her side. After the usual custom, they were served on a single bread trencher that was placed between them. The man was supposed to carve the meat with his dagger and offer his lady her portion. The bread trencher was a hard-baked slab of bread with a raised rim to catch and contain the gravies and juices of the meats served on it. After the meal the trenchers were customarily given to the dogs that brawled under the tables or distributed to the beggars who always flocked outside a castle gate at dinnertime.

The talk was agitated at the great U-shaped collection of tables that flanked three walls of the hall. The sound of the lute player was almost drowned out as men and women babbled on of recent triumphs and future victory. With so many men oversea, there was always one or even more women for every man of Falcon's. Marie knew that she had to look forward to a good many births next summer. Meanwhile, though, she was feeling safe and protected, if not quite secure, for the first time since her father had left for Outremer, leaving the keeping of castle and land in her hands.

Draco reached into a venison pie, fished out a hunk of savory meat, and wrapped it in a piece of crust. He handed the morsel to Marie, and she bit into it, leaning out far over the trencher, so that the juices would not drip onto her velvet gown. The juices ran over her fingers and down her chin, but she carefully blotted her lips and chin with her damask napkin, as well-bred ladies were supposed to do.

She dipped her fingers in the bowl of water next to her and accepted the cup of wine that Falcon handed her. In former times, a single huge cup had been passed from hand to hand for all to drink from, but now, in refined company, each couple shared a cup between them. She watched as Falcon gnawed a bone of boar ham clean but for scraps and tossed it to the dogs that rooted in the musty straw covering the floor. A fierce fight immediately broke out and the watchers cheered the combatants on until a bloody-snouted mastiff finally made off with the prize.

"Keep an eye on that yellow bitch there," shouted Falcon to Marie's dog keeper. "She'll throw you many a fine, strong pup!" The dog keeper nodded vigorous agreement.

"You seem in fine spirits tonight, Sir Draco," Marie said.

"I have to be," he said, smiling broadly. "We are still in a poor position, and I can't let my men know it."

"What?" Marie gasped, dismayed. "With the fine force you've trained? I had thought the problem of Thibaut all but settled."

"Not at all, my lady," Falcon said. "These are good men, but they are not yet nearly as well trained as they think they are. That will take many more months. Their quality and the training they have received so far counts for much, but it still falls short of overcoming a four-to-one superiority in numbers. You may emphasize individual superiority as much as you like, but sheer weight of numbers is still the deciding factor on the field."

"You can wager on it, my lady," said Wulf, who was occupied with a haunch of venison on the side of Marie opposite to Falcon's. "Four footmen, even if they be only half trained, can bring down the finest knight who ever swung a sword. Especially," he added, "if they know how to use the spear." The Saxon was a bit drunk but spoke with the authority of a man who knew his trade. Marie's spirits sank.

"Even so," Falcon continued, "I would not worry, considering the quality of your cousin and his leadership."

"That's true," said Marie, brightening. "Thibaut's a coward and a fool and can give you little trouble."

"Unfortunately," Falcon said, "Thibaut is not in command of Thibaut's troops. Gunther Valdemar is. And Gunther Valdemar is one of the finest, most cunning professional soldiers who ever took the field in Outremer."

"And *that*," Wulf said, "you may also wager on, my lady." The Saxon broke open a steaming bread roll, scooped up two fingers full of butter from a tub, and spread the butter on the bread, which he then thrust into his mouth.

Her ladies helped Marie peel out of the tight velvet gown. On an impulse, she ordered hot water and bathed in the big carved stone tub that sat in the tiny room opening off her chamber. The women brought in steaming pitchers of hot water from the kitchen to mix with the water that was piped down from the cistern on the roof. Extravagantly, Marie sprinkled mineral salts from Outremer into the water. She soaked for a long time, luxuriating in the silky scented liquid and absorbing its fragrance into her pores. Her ladies scrubbed her pale skin until it glowed, and when she stood, dripping, they rubbed her down with rough towels until she tingled from hairline to toenails. She ordered a clean shift brought from her chest, and the garment of Egyptian cotton, scented with the cedar of the chest and the herbs and rose petals it had been packed away with, was drawn down over her body. She dismissed her attendants then, bidding them leave her a pitcher of the fine stolen wine. . . . and two goblets.

She did not know why she knew that this was the night, but she knew it, as naturally as she knew the path of her monthly cycle.

His knock came after her ladies had left and the candle by the bed had burned down a half inch. She had expected a violent pounding, but it was oddly hesitant, almost like that of a young man approaching his first mistress.

"Come in," she said, a huskiness in her voice that she had not suspected before.

The door creaked open. He was not in the same clothes he had been wearing at dinner, and she could not restrain a small sigh of relief to see that his hair was wet. He too had bathed before coming to her.

Falcon closed the door behind him, then bolted it, then unstrapped his sword and left it leaning against the door. He reached the bed in two long strides and sat on its edge.

"Marie?" he said, and her arms reached up to him and his lips came down on hers. Their tongues circled each other, exploring the interiors of their mouths. Marie broke away and sighed as his hand touched her face, then slid down her neck, her shoulder, glided over and then cupped her breast, making the nipple harden, then moved down again to her waist. She shivered slightly when his gentle caresses lingered on her belly, then rested briefly at the joining of her thighs and then, before she could gasp, traced her ripe curves once more to her knee.

She was trying to muster words when his lips came down on hers again and his hand came back up, and this time he untied the laces of her shift and threw it open. The hand retraced its former path, only this time it roamed over bare flesh instead of touching the cotton shift. Her breath grew shallow and irregular. "My lord . . ." She shuddered.

"I think you can call me Draco now," he said, but his voice was not as steady as he had intended.

"My lord," she repeated, thrusting her belly up against his hand, forcing it lower. She tore his mouth from hers and with her hand behind his head forced his lips down to her breast. Her other hand roamed his body, seeking and stroking all the hard, angular places.

Abruptly, he tore away from her and stood. She almost whimpered in disappointment until she realized that he was tearing off his clothes. He ripped his tunic loose, then stripped his hose down to his feet and stood naked before her in the candlelight.

His body was as perfect as a god's, but it shared the peculiarities of his face. The skin was perfectly white, and the line which was white on his face and neck continued as a thin pink tracery down his chest, tracing a white streak through the thick black hair that curled there, continuing down his belly to his groin, turning the pubic hair on the left side a similar white. The line continued down the inside of the left thigh, thence down the calf to the heel. Her eyes in following the bizarre line with its path of white hair had passed the juncture of his thighs almost without noticing what was there, but her attention was drawn back soon enough.

"Draco! how did that hap—" Her words were cut off as his weight descended upon her and she felt the full length of his body on her own and his tongue claimed hers again. She opened her legs and tried to maneuver him between them, but he put his hands on her shoulders and pushed her back onto her pillows.

"Plenty of time for that, my love," he said. There was a new light in his eyes, unlike the extremes of mirth or fury or depression that she had seen there before. It was a mild, gentle, sensuous light, faintly mocking and infinitely self-indulgent. She lay back to accept what he would give.

She writhed for a long time under the stroking of his hands. They explored, touched, teased, with a knowledge and surety that her troubador had never possessed. He could touch a spot that she had thought her own special secret, and draw forth a response more intense than anything she had ever imagined.

She tried to match his expertise as she matched his ardor, touching and stroking the hard length of him, cupping the weighty, pendulous mass that hung below, but she really did not know quite what to do. In the end, though, it made no difference, because he led her through all the steps she needed to know. She was amazed when he made her lie back with her hands grasping frantically at the bedstead while his lips roamed down her neck to linger on her breasts, then down across her belly. She writhed as his tongue darted into her navel, but his powerful hand held her down as his lips roved across her belly, to kiss the insides of her thighs, to center on the furry juncture between them.

She needed to scream, and he let her, for in the thick-walled interior of a castle, no sound could be heard from one room to the next. She welcomed his penetration with a relief she would not have believed possible a day before. Once she had believed this the totality of the act, but now she knew it to be only a delicious stage in a process which began much earlier and, she was sure, would extend far beyond.

She tried to keep calm, to savor this experience which might well never happen again. But the waves of sensation radiated from the joining of their bodies to her head and she set her teeth into his shoulder and gave vent to a last, muffled, shuddering scream as her interior seemed to dissolve and rearrange into a new and entirely more satisfactory pattern.

At the same moment, she felt Draco stiffen. He pushed himself up from her on his hands, his face twisted into a flushed, rigid mask, his breath wheezing in a manner that would have been alarming under any other circumstances. He drove himself so deep that it was painful, but she enjoyed even the pain. She felt the jerking of his body that signified what was happening within her, then he collapsed in a sweaty, heaving mass upon her similarly sweltering body.

It had been ecstasy. She also knew that she had committed a terrible sin, but she was sure that eternity in hell was a reasonable price to pay for what she had just experienced.

And would experience again tomorrow night, if she had anything to say about it.

The candle was half gone. In its pale light, Falcon admired the graceful curve of Marie's back where it dipped in toward her waist before soaring once again into the arc of her hip. He ran a hand appreciatively along the winsome curve and she sighed contentedly, lying face down, her hair spread over her shoulders and the pillow.

Falcon took her shoulder and rolled her over toward him.

"Not again, my love," she said sleepily. "You can't be . . . What's that?" She pointed to the narrow, slit window, through which a flickering, ruddy light was beginning to glare. Falcon leaped to his feet and climbed up onto the chest below the window. He leaned out over the broad sill, where the narrow window widened. The windows were narrow to keep out missiles, and widened inside to allow archers to traverse their weapons. Falcon could see men rushing across the bailey to the main gate, which was beginning to burn.

"God's teeth!" Falcon barked, dashing for the door. "I should have guessed it! That bastard Valdemar's mounted a night attack." He snatched up his sword in its scabbard and threw the bolts back and jerked the door open. Bellowing for his men, he dashed down the stair to the hall.

Clutching a sheet to her body, Marie ran to the door and leaned out. "But Draco," she shouted after him, "your clothes!"

Men were beginning to rouse from their sleep in the straw of the hall floor. The clamor from outside was beginning to penetrate, and they blinked in amazement at the sight of their captain striding across the hall with his great Saracen sword in his hand, stark naked.

"To arms!" he thundered. "Grab your weapons and follow me! Bring torches, or we'll be killing one another. It's a night attack." Most were confused. Night attacks were almost unheard of in these parts.

Falcon burst through the door and into the bailey. Three figures were silhouetted against the flaming ruins of the gate, holding it against all comers. On the left, Falcon could make out Wulf with his falchion and buckler. On the right was Donal with his ax. In the center was a Spanish knight called Sir Ruy Ortiz. The other two were in their hose, but Ruy was in full armor and swinging the broad blade he called Moorslayer with both hands. Beyond them many figures were illuminated by the flames, trying to get close enough to ply their spears.

On the walk that ran below the top of the wall flanking the gate, Rupert Foul-Mouth stood, calmly calling out advice and vituperation. In his hand was a massive wooden maul, a huge-headed hammer for driving stakes. From time to time a head would appear above the parapet, and Rupert would smash it back down.

" 'Ware that monkey-bugger to your left, Wulf, me lad. Take that, you shit-sucking toad fucker! Mind your right, Ruy, there's a nun-buggering daggerman after your cods!"

Falcon reached the gate. "Step through and spread! I'm coming through." Obediently, the other three stepped out beneath the gate lintel into the midst of their attackers, who fell back momentarily in astonishment at the unexpected action. Then Falcon was through, swinging Nemesis in hissing arcs, each of which removed an enemy from the fight. Wulf howled like his namesake beast with joy to see his master in the battle, and Donal yelled wild Gaelic war cries while Ruy called on St. James.

Never taking his attention from the men before him, Falcon scanned the area flanking the gates. Men were hurling burning bundles of sticks against the timber palisade, but having a little luck. Since putting the castle on a war footing Falcon had had the timber wall doused with water daily. The gate must have burned because the enemy had had time to stack oil-soaked wood against it. What had become of the sentries?

Falcon cursed at the pain in his feet where he had trod on burning cinders when he came through the gate. Two men wielding glaives—long, curved cutting blades on poles—closed on Falcon, and he had brisk work for a few seconds, removing an arm from one and cutting the feet from under the other while avoiding the whirring blades.

A horseman tried to ride Falcon down, swinging an ax

at his unprotected head. Nemesis took the hand off at the wrist and Falcon grabbed the armored bicep as the man sagged forward in shock and hauled him from the saddle. He got a scorched foot into a stirrup and heaved himself into the saddle. It was an awkward move for a man grasping a sword, but he managed it and went riding wildly among the enemy, whooping and shouting.

"Valdemar! Valdemar! Where are you, German pig? Show yourself!" A lancer rode at him, and he halved the man with a horizontal slash. The lance had not even come close. In the uncertain light of the flames, Falcon could not use his customary artistic cuts, and Nemesis wreaked truly awesome carnage in wild sweeps that sheared through armor as if it were cloth. Soon, men were avoiding the incredible naked horseman and Falcon heard some shouting that he was not a man but a night goblin come to defend La Roche.

Then he saw Valdemar. The coif and nose piece of his helmet obscured most of his face, but there was no mistaking the huge yellow mustache that drooped almost to his chest. The German was sitting his horse calmly on a slight rise of ground to the rear and slightly to one side of the action.

Falcon wheeled his horse for a charge at Valdemar, but at that moment the German raised his hands and thirty armored knights in tight formation thundered at the gate, lances lowered. They were going to force a way through now that the fire had subsided a little, and they charged on a front five horses wide, six ranks deep.

"Back through the gate!" Falcon shouted. He had no time to wheel his horse and escape, so he stood in his stirrups, Nemesis held high above his head, determined to sell his life dearly.

Without warning, the front rank of horsemen collapsed, and Falcon had a brief glimpse of a horse going down with a crossbow bolt lodged in its brow. The next line crashed into the first, and then the whole charge was piling up into the tangle of bodies of man and horse. More bolts sang into the confused mass, and then Falcon could see the yard-long arrows of the Welsh bows, and the rate of fire from the longbows was far greater than that of the crossbows.

Falcon could hear Valdemar's rage-strangled bellows, and gradually the attackers fell back, leaving their wounded on the field. Falcon's men, armed now, began pouring out through the gate.

"Don't pursue!" Falcon shouted. "Just hold the gate. If you give chase, they'll pick you off one by one."

Valdemar's force faded back into the darkness, and soon the only sounds were those of crackling fires and the groans of the wounded. When he was sure that no further attack was imminent, Falcon dismounted.

"Who was on guard?" He called. The Spanish knight, Ruy Ortiz, came forward.

"I was captain of the watch, my lord. There were two spearmen at the gate, up there on the wallwalk, when I inspected after supper. I made a full circuit of the bailey along the wallwalk and no post had anything to report. When I got back, I saw the gate was burning. My calls roused Wulf and Donal, and we held them off as the gate came down."

"You did well, Ruy. It was my fault for not posting a stronger watch."

"But, my lord," protested the knight, "who would have thought of a night attack? In Spain, even the Moors seldom try that."

"Valdemar would, and I should have known it." He raised his voice to a shout. "Where are the gate sentries?"

After a few moments' searching among the bodies, Wulf and Donal arrived, dragging two corpses by the heels. Falcon called for torches. Wulf squatted by his lord to examine the necks of the unfortunate spearmen and he pointed to a thin line of red encircling the neck of each.

"That was done by a Saracen bowstring garrote," Wulf said. Falcon cursed luridly.

"Valdemar didn't return alone from Outremer."

"Assassins?" asked Ruy. At the word, there was much fearful muttering and making of the sign of the cross and gestures against the evil eye from the men standing within earshot. Assassins, fanatical killers of the Isamaili sect formed by the dreaded Old Man of the Mountain in Outremer, were known to have supernatural powers conferred upon them by Satan for the murder of Christians.

"No, not Assassins," Falcon said, straightening. "Assassins favor the dagger. This was done by ordinary desert fighters, Berbers, most likely. They're all cunning at night work."

Rupert came up to Falcon and handed him a wineskin. Falcon accepted it gratefully and took a long pull, soothing his parched throat. His feet were beginning to sting abominably.

"Thy cock's all adangle, my lord," Rupert said. "Shall I fetch your clothes?"

"No. Form up the men. I want to address them." If the old engineer was surprised, he concealed it well and went shouting to rally the soldiers, adding many pertinent details concerning their ancestry and habits. The men lined up raggedly, and Falcon strode up and down the line as if conducting a routine inspection. The men strove not to stare at their naked, blood-splashed leader, who swung the dripping sword idly in his fist.

"I hope you understand, now," Falcon began, "how much you have to learn yet. For what happened tonight, I take full responsibility. You fought as well as might be expected." The men flushed with shame at the faint praise, which was worse than a tongue-lashing. "From now on," Falcon continued, "we will hold night training. There will be no more heavy wine-drinking at supper.

Men scheduled for sentry duty at night will have no wine at all after noon." Faces fell with dismay. Falcon pointed at the two corpses.

"Two of your comrades are dead because they were too full of wine to hear a couple of Saracen stranglers creeping up the wall on ropes and grapples. We almost all died as a result." The men looked more subdued. The thought of black-faced heathens creeping about and strangling honest soldiers filled them with superstitious dread.

"Another thing," Falcon shouted. He pointed at the few men who bore arms and were as naked as he or dressed only in their hose, in which they had probably slept. "Those men behaved rightly. This is how you tell a true warrior from a play-actor. When he is roused by an alarm in the night, a true warrior reaches for his weapons before he reaches for his clothes. And keep your footgear by your side in the night." He looked down at his own burned feet. "I didn't this night, and I'll pay for it tomorrow and for some days to come."

The men received their chastisement well. It pleased them that their master took the trouble to tell them what they had done wrong, instead of merely cursing and flogging them, as most would have done. That he admitted his own faults in the matter almost surpassed belief. It told them that he was a soldier as they were soldiers, and that he intended to improve himself as well as them.

"Ruy," he called, "turn the guard mount over to Rudolph of Austria and turn in. You've had a hard night." He turned to a burly, red-haired man who was one of those who had not dressed. "Rudolph, take a full half of the men and post them. Arm yourself and get a gang of the working men together to block that gate. Rupert can help you with that." The Austrian touched his brow in acknowledgment and went in search of his armor. "That's all," Falcon called. "Turn out for drill at first light. Dismissed." Limping now, Falcon walked back to the keep, where a gaggle of ladies and serving girls who had gathered at the door fled shrieking at the approach of the naked knight. Not, however, without first sneaking a long, close look.

A knot of men, including Rupert, Donal, and Wulf, stood around a horse trough, washing the swiftly clotting blood from their weapons and calling to the serving boys for rags and oil.

"Well," Donal said, "which was it?"

"Aye," chuckled Rupert, "his lordship's parts were a bit shiny when he came charging like a bare-arsed pagan idol into the fray. One of the serving wenches? Or one of my lady's maids?" A quick consultation was held, and it was soon established that every woman attractive enough to have caught Draco Falcon's eye had been claimed that night by one of them. All but one.

"Oh, aye," said Rupert, with a lewd cackle, "I'll warrant that Lady Marie de Cleves was on her knees a-praying to St. Peter this night!"

SIX

ARCHBISHOP Fulcher was annoyed. He sat slowly turning his jeweled goblet in plump hands while Thibaut unreeled the list of his woes. They had had a profitable arrangement until recently. Thibaut had had the wit to confine his depredations to small, easily taken fiefs near his lands or carving away digestible chunks of larger lands whose masters were away. For a percentage of the takings, Fulcher saw to it that complaints about the sacrilege got no higher than the offices of his own archepiscopal see, where they were filed away, never to reach Rome.

Then Thibaut had let his greed exceed his severely limited capabilities. He had hired the horrendous German knight whose attitudes paled even Fulcher's hardened cynicism. The German was ruthless and capable and had begun rolling up Crusaders' lands at an alarming rate. Now they were even attacking the land of Bertrand de Cleves, a much-beloved baron long in Saracen captivity. And this day Fulcher had received alarming news.

"I don't understand it!" Thibaut was lamenting. "I trusted Sir Gunther to brush away this petty adventurer from Outremer and bend my pretty cousin to my will. He mounted a brilliant night attack against her little fort, and what was the result? Thirty of my men killed, and ten horses lost, and much arms and equipment. He was able to report only two of this Draco's men killed for sure. My men say that the knight with the white streak rode among them stark naked, swinging a great curved sword. Naked as he was, no weapon could touch him. Men clearly saw a lance bend around him before it could run him through. They say that purple flames shot from the horse's nostrils."

Fulcher felt a tremble of fear. He had little respect left for God, but there were other powers. "Do you think he is in league with Satan? Was it a black horse? It is said that the Prince of Darkness often takes the form of a black horse to aid his minions." Both men crossed themselves at mention of the dread lord.

"You two prattle like maidens in a bower," said Valdemar from where he was sitting and drinking from a huge cup. "The horse was one he took from one of my own knights, and the only flames thereabouts were the ones we set. He prevailed because, naked or armored, he is the best fighter in these parts save myself."

"Then why did you not do combat with him?" Thibaut demanded.

"Because I'm not such a fool as to engage an unknown enemy in the dark. It leaves too much to chance, and double kills often result, profiting nobody. That was the main reason for the attack anyway. I wished to see the quality of my enemy, and I did."

"A costly lesson, sir knight!" Thibaut fumed.

"Thirty men?" Valdemar shrugged his huge shoulders and made a rude, deprecating noise with his lips. "What is cheaper than men?"

"But the horses!" Thibaut yelled. "And the arms! Have you no thought for those?"

"My lords," said Fulcher soothingly, "pray cease this bickering. There are far more serious matters afoot. I have received this day word from Rome."

"From Rome?" said Thibaut with dread.

"Yes. What I knew would happen has occurred. Word of the disturbances here has reached the Holy See. When your sackings grew intolerably great, the rumors finally trickled to Rome. I strongly suspect the abbot of the monastery at Les Sources."

"I should have killed that fool on the road when we met Draco for the first time!" fumed Thibaut. Valdemar barked a short laugh.

"You were lucky to escape with your own life from that affray, my lord." The way Valdemar spoke the honorific, it was an insult. "Leave the killing to me and stick to counting your money."

"My lords," Fulcher went on, "this is most serious! I could have my see confiscated."

"Oh, most serious indeed," Valdemar said sarcastically. "Well, speak on, little bishop."

"A papal inspector is on his way to investigate the happenings hereabouts. He is a certain Cardinal Eusebius, and he is empowered with full authority to judge in the matter."

"A papal legate has no temporal power," the German said. "We've touched no church property, so he can't complain to the king of that."

"He can excommunicate my lord Thibaut and dispossess me!" the archbishop said.

"My lord Thibaut's soul is his own concern. If we lose you, we shall console ourselves with the thought that your replacement will probably be equally cooperative."

"But Valdemar!" Thibaut fretted. "If I'm excommunicated, I'll die unshriven! No Christian can offer me hospitality or refuge and I'll be an outcast."

Valdemar snorted his contempt. "I've known excommunicates all over Christendom, and they fared no worse than other men. Kings and emperors have been excommunicated and been none the worse for it. Just send a contrite letter and a handsome gift to the Pope and he'll come to terms. He'll shrive you and assign a nice pilgrimage as penance and we can go on robbing your neighbors as before. It needn't even come to that. If this cardinal is like most of the others I've known, he'll appreciate the clink of gold as much as the archbishop here."

Fulcher flushed deeply. "Not this cardinal. Eusebius is a Spaniard, and a fanatic at rooting out sin and heresy. He treats every offense with severity and is most unforgiving of anything he thinks to reflect dishonor on the church.

"More than that, he is bringing a *pacata* with him."

"A what?" asked Valdemar.

"It's something I've not heard of in this generation," Fulcher said, "but a pacata is a military force organized to enforce the Truce of God upon rebellious Christians. At their head is a churchman, and they owe fealty only to the Pope." This was heavy news indeed. To resist such a force was to take up arms against the church itself. Neighboring barons would delight in the chance to band together and carve up Thibaut's domains with the blessings of Holy Mother Church.

"We must consider this," Valdemar said, his calm in contrast to the agitation of the other two. "There may be a way of turning even this to account."

Falcon examined the morningstar. Simon had taken it to the smith and had it slightly altered. The ball was studded all over with two-inch iron spikes, but he had had the smith remove the spike opposite the point where the chain was joined to the ball and had substituted for it an extra long spike of perhaps five inches.

"It's for a trick Donal taught me," the ex-monk explained. "You see, most men expect you to start the ball whirling before you fight, so as to keep it under control. Now watch." Simon stood about four feet in front of the practice post, the morningstar dangling limply from his hand. With a snap of the wrist, he brought the handle of the weapon up sharply to waist level and halted it there. The ball on the end of its chain shot forward and up and the long spike sank into the post at the level of the throat. Simon smiled with pride as he pulled the ball loose.

"Excellent!" Falcon said. "I'll have to remember that one." He was, of course, familiar with the trick, but he was pleased with Simon's swift and growing mastery of the extremely difficult weapon. And the idea of the long spike was a good one, turning a maneuver designed to gain a momentary advantage into a deadly trick. "Keep it up. I'll set you to training the others soon."

There was a commotion at the bailey gate, newly rebuilt, and Falcon went to see what was happening. It was a messenger dressed in the livery of a high churchman's servant, unarmed but booted and spurred like a knight, except that the spurs were of plain steel and not gold-plated or gilded. In a gloved hand the man carried a folded parchment. "I seek the Lady Marie de Cleves and her captain, Sir Draco Falcon."

"I'm Falcon," Draco said. Marie came to the gate, and the two conducted the man to the keep. Inside, when he had been given refreshment, he handed the packet to Marie. She looked at its seal.

"I don't know this seal," she said.

"It is that of the Cardinal Eusebius, my lady," said the messenger. "Shall I read it for you?"

"My captain can read," she said, handing the message to Falcon. The messenger studied him with interest. A literate knight was worth looking at. Falcon cut the string with his dagger and removed the seal. He read the message aloud, for the art of reading silently was as yet unknown. The message summoned Marie and Falcon, along with Thibaut and Valdemar, to a church court to be held in the nearby town of St. Rémy, the very town where Falcon had met Marie. There they were to be examined to determine whether any of the parties fell under church ban for violating the Truce of God.

"What does this word *pacata* mean?" Falcon asked. The messenger explained. Falcon looked at Marie.

"What are your wishes, my lady? If you wish my advice, I say that you have been attacked while your father was on Crusade, and the right is entirely on your side."

"If that is the case, my lady, then you need have no fear of an unfavorable judgment," the messenger said.

"My lady will make her own decision," Falcon said. "And, my lady, I do not feel that you should assume that you will receive justice from a church court."

"Sir, I protest!" the messenger said. "You come close to blasphemy!"

Falcon stared at the man with cold eyes. "I know how the church defines blasphemy, and I may think and say what I like about her minions without fear of transgression. I know what Archbishop Fulcher is. Why should this Cardinal Eusebius be any different?" Then Marie placed a hand on his shoulder.

"No, Sir Draco, I think we should go. Whatever the cardinal is like, a record of the proceedings will go to Rome. The facts of what has happened here will become public knowledge. Thus even if we fail and Thibaut prevails"—she looked down and paused at the terrible thought—"then, when my father returns from his captivity, he will have that as evidence when he sues for the return of his land."

"Perhaps you're right, my lady," Falcon said dubiously. "But we go with all our men, and all armed."

"Convey my respects to the cardinal," Marie said to

the messenger. "And tell him that we will be before him on the appointed day."

Cardinal Eusebius was a middle-aged man with a severe, ascetic face framed by his white linen coif. His voluminous crimson robes spread out over his throne, and a wide red hat shaded his eyes. He wore red gloves with small white crosses on their backs. He studied the defendants before him with impartial eyes.

He had been listening to their stories all day. It had been obvious from the first who was at fault. The man Thibaut was the kind of greedy, sneaking, cowardly nobleman that Europe abounded in, since all worthy men had taken the cross. His collusion with Archbishop Fulcher was also obvious. That churchman's modest see could not have supported the splendor in which the man lived—the fine horses, the beautiful hawks, the country houses and hunting lodges. Eusebius had arrived sooner than expected, and Fulcher had not had time to hide his wealth.

Marie de Cleves seemed a fine lady, forced like many to manage the family possessions in the absence of her menfolk. The local people had nothing but good to say of her. She was the natural prey of such as Thibaut. If it were not for the damnable lack of evidence! For each of his seizures of land, Thibaut claimed aggression or produced documents to indicate his prior ownership. The papers were almost certainly forgeries, but that would take much time to prove.

The two captains were another matter. A pair of sell-swords, of a type becoming alarmingly common of late. They were little better than hired bravos and professional murderers, but both had splendid records in the Crusade. The cardinal sighed with frustration. Why could Christian fighting men not confine their belligerent activities to the Holy Land, and leave Christendom to heal its ancient wounds in peace? Didn't the church have enough problems with all the heretical sects that were springing up without having to settle the disputes of petty barons who behaved like bandits?

Both sides had brought their armies, so many men that the court had to be held in a field outside the city walls instead of in the town square as Eusebius had wanted. A wooden platform had been erected for him to enthrone himself, much decorated with colored cloths and with guardsmen holding his personal banner and that of the Pope. His *pacata* stood between the force of the two disputants—three hundred men, each a hardened warrior with many years in Outremer behind him. They were sergeants upon whom their special service conveyed the status of knights. Each was splendidly mounted and armed, and they were a match for an ordinary feudal levy of much larger size.

The cardinal raised a gloved hand for silence, and the crowd from the city that had gathered to gawk at the novel spectacle was quickly stilled. "Hear my judgment in this matter. The charges are grave; charges meriting excommunication and exile. Both sides have sworn a holy oath of innocence. The evidence is not sufficient to merit a judgment on the basis of its quality." There were smiles from Thibaut and Valdemar. "Therefore," Eusebius went on, "God must decide. There are three ways to determine guilt and innocence in such a case.

"First: the trial by ordeal of fire. Each defendant must take up in the naked hand a bar of glowing hot iron and hold it for the space of ten heartbeats. After three days the bandages shall be removed and the burns examined. If the burn is healing cleanly, then the defendant is innocent. If it festers, then the defendant is guilty.

"Second: the ordeal of water. Each defendant shall be cast into deep water. If the defendant sinks beneath the water, then he is innocent. If he floats, then he is being borne up by demons and must be adjudged guilty.

"Third: the trial by combat. The defendant or a chosen champion will engage in single combat to the death and God will choose between them. Choose."

"Combat!" said all four voices at once. Eusebius had expected no less. In all his years as a papal judge, no one had ever chosen fire or water.

"Very well," Eusebius said. "Since the Lady Marie de Cleves is a woman, she must choose a champion to fight for her cause."

"My captain, Draco Falcon, shall do battle for me," Marie said. Draco smiled at her and folded his arms.

"My Lord Thibaut," Eusebius said, "will you fight your own cause?"

"As your eminence can see," Thibaut said, "God has seen fit to test my faith with a wasting disease of the leg, and to deform my shoulder, a rare privilege for which I am humbly grateful." Eusebius struggled to keep a straight face at the mealy-mouthed protestation. "This debility has forced me to forgo the practice of arms and the taking of the cross which I so ardently desired. My captain, the great Crusader Gunther Valdemar, will do battle for me."

"Very well," Eusebius said. He looked at the position of the sun, which had moved only a little way past its noontime high. "There is sufficient time to decide this matter today. Gentlemen, prepare yourselves. Do you wish a priest to hear your confessions and give you communion?"

"Let's not fritter away our time," Valdemar said. "I'm ready as soon as I can arm." Falcon shrugged his indifference.

"Quite aside from the merits of this case," Eusebius said, "you are a pair of miscreants, despite all your glory in Outremer. Go arm yourselves. The defendants may join me upon this dais to witness the judgment of God."

Falcon walked to where his men waited. He had had to attend the court unarmed, and he felt as naked as he had been on the night of the attack. The audience was frantic with excitement at the prospect of a trial by combat. Such a thing hadn't been seen in this town in many years, and never had anyone seen a duel between two great champions! This would be a thing worth telling to one's grandchildren.

Wulf helped his master on with the padded leather doublet, then the coat of mail, then the helmet. When he was satisfied that everything was secured properly, Falcon mounted and his long, triangular shield was handed up to him. He slipped his arm through the straps and adjusted it. Next, he took up the long ash pole of his lance and was ready to do battle. He rode to the dais and halted before the cardinal. Marie sat on the cardinal's right, Thibaut on his left. Marie wore a worried frown, Thibaut a confident smirk.

Valdemar, now fully armed, rode up. His equipment was much like Falcon's. His hauberk, instead of having the fine Saracen links of Falcon's armor, was made of hammered iron rings of exceptional thickness. It would be extremely hard to cut, and a man as powerful as Valdemar did not mind the extra weight.

The cardinal stood and signaled for silence once more. "You fight as champions for the defendants before this court. Will you strive, with lance and sword, to defend with your bodies the claims of your lieges, until God rewards with victory the side which is just?"

"We will!" shouted both.

"Then go forth to do battle. He that prevails is in the right. He that asks quarter shall be adjudged recreant, and degraded from the status of knighthood. If one is slain, then the slayer shall be innocent of his blood, for this is the judgment of God."

The champions had begun to turn to ride to their ends of the field when Thibaut raised an arm and cried: "Your eminence, I protest!"

"What is this?" Eusebius said, "Surely you don't wish to take the field yourself, Lord Thibaut?" There was raucous laughter from the watchers, which the cardinal silenced with a glare.

Thibaut had been expecting the judgment of trial by combat, and Valdemar had carefully coached him for this speech.

"Your eminence, what I protest is the sword that the bravo Draco Falcon bears. It is a Saracen sword."

"What of it?" the cardinal said testily. "Half the men who return from Outremer carry Saracen blades, and there have been no complaints thus far."

"That is true, your eminence, but they have those swords rehilted with decent Christian cross-hilts. I have seen that sword used, and it has properties that can only be the result of supernatural aid. It cleaves armor with the ease of a sharp knife going through venison. Look at the hilt and pommel," he said, pointing. "They both are in the form of the crescent moon, and who among us is ignorant of the fact that the crescent is the symbol of the devil-worshiping heathen of Outremer?"

There was a murmur of superstitious awe throughout the onlookers, and necks were craned to get a look at the terrible blade. The cardinal stood in thought for a few moments.

"This is a valid objection," he said at length. "Sir Draco, if you wish to use that sword, you must have an armorer rehilt it with a cross-hilt. Perhaps also with a saint's relic in the pommel, to take off any heathen curse."

"The sword stays as it is!" said Draco sternly.

"Then you must use another," said the cardinal, re-seating himself.

Draco spared a scowling glare for Valdemar before turning once again to ride back to his men. The German just smiled, then he wheeled his horse and rode laughing to his end of the field.

"Ruy Ortiz," Falcon shouted, "lend me Moorslayer!" The Spanish knight ran forward, unbuckling his belt, while Wulf unfastened Nemesis's belt and scabbard. He removed Falcon's dagger from the belt and transferred it to Ruy's. When it was securely belted about him, Falcon drew Moorslayer and whirled it about his head, getting its feel. It had been a long time since he had wielded the long, straight knightly sword, but he had been drilled long, hard, and early in its use. Moorslayer pleased him with its extra length and width. Except for Nemesis, it was the longest sword in the company.

"She will not fail you, my lord. It is an honor to me that you choose her." Falcon resheathed the blade.

Slowly he trotted his horse up and down to assure himself that the stallion was in good fettle. The he turned to face Valdemar. They were separated by about three hundred paces.

Falcon began walking his destrier forward. Valdemar did the same. There was no sound but the slow clop of the horses' hooves, muffled by the grass. At two hundred paces, both broke into a trot. Each man held his lance loosely, arm held slack to take up the spring of his horse's motion.

At one hundred paces, both horses surged into a gallop. As the motion of his horse smoothed out, Falcon snapped his lance down to the horizontal position, gripping the shaft tightly under his arm and aiming it straight for Valdemar's eyes. Valdemar's lance was held identically.

The horses were closing now. Falcon stood in his stirrups, horse and man welded into a single unit, the entire weight of beast and man and iron concentrated on the tip of the lance, for a thousand years the most remorseless engine of destruction ever devised. Falcon held his shield close to his body, raised so that only his eyes showed above its upper rim.

At the last instant, just as they were about to meet, Falcon braced himself and jerked his shield up the last half inch to protect his eyes. He felt the tremendous impact of Valdemar's lance meeting his shield. This was the instant for which all knights trained half their lives. If his own lance was not also perfectly placed, he would almost certainly die at the next instant.

There was a tremendous roar from the crowd at the shock of lance on shield. The two horsemen seemed to stop for a frozen instant, then they were riding past one another, and the sound of the two lances snapping was audible for half a mile. The cheering of the crowd was frantic, and mixed in with it was a scream. So powerful had been the impact that a jagged splinter of lance shaft a foot long had flown a hundred yards and impaled the shoulder of a peasant standing on the sidelines. Nobody paid any attention to the trifling incident except the unfortunate peasant himself.

On the dais, Marie had closed her eyes at the instant of collision, only to be further terrified at the sound of the shivering lances. Surely no human being could survive such a shock! At the sound of the cheering, she opened her eyes and let out a relieved sigh. He was still alive. Thibaut gnawed worriedly at his lower lip. So far, so good.

"Valdemar will have him at the next pass," he said.

Even Cardinal Eusebius was enthralled. He found himself with a new understanding of the old Romans and the terrible games that St. Augustine had so condemned. Surely there was nothing so thrilling as combat between true champions. And it served a purpose. Whoever won, there would be one less brawler to plague Christendom this night.

As he wheeled his horse to ride back, Falcon tore Moorslayer from its scabbard. His shield still seemed to be sound, but he couldn't see the front and tell for sure. His whole body ached from absorbing the shock of Valdemar's lance. He'd come close to being unseated. A man on foot while his opponent was still mounted faced almost certain death.

Valdemar shook himself and checked his shield. Four inches of lance point protruded from its back. That might be a nuisance later on. The man he was sharing the field with was a matchless jouster, no question of it, but the German was not terribly worried. He had weighted the odds in his favor by tricking Falcon into fighting with an unfamiliar sword, and he had other advantages thoughtfully laid out ahead of time, in anticipation of this combat. He drew his sword, Helm-Cleaver, from its sheath. Time for another pass. He spurred for his enemy.

Falcon raised his shield and rode for the German knight. Each held his sword far back for the overhand swing. The knightly long sword was useless for thrusting, and it was difficult to wield in short cuts or chops. A weighty, massive weapon, it was swung in great circles pivoting at the user's shoulder. It was the terrible momentum built up by this long sweep, backed by the muscle of a powerful warrior, that made the long sword such a deadly weapon, and it was against this weapon that a knight's protective equipment was designed. An unarmored man or one without a helmet or one whose shield was not at least rimmed with iron stood little chance.

As the two horses came together, the light of the sun flashed on the twin arcs of the swords and the great shout went up again as sword met shield. Falcon raised his shield, to have it smashed back against the nasal of his helmet. At the same instant, the crash of his own sword against Valdemar's shield sent a shock from his wrist to his shoulder. He could feel Moorslayer sinking into something, and he hoped it was Valdemar's head.

Then the horses were apart again. Falcon gripped Moorslayer tightly as the blade tore free of whatever it had been embedded in. To his bitter disappointment, it had merely sunk its edge into the rim of Valdemar's shield. All around the field, the experienced knights cheered and chattered with one another in appreciation. One was seldom privileged to see two such masterly passes in succession. Surely the next must be fatal.

Once more, the two horses approached. This time, as Falcon swung Moorslayer, Valdemar leaned low and to one side. Jerking his mailed foot from his stirrup, he kicked Falcon's horse in the mouth. Falcon was carried forward and off balance as he strove to check his blow, and the horse reared in surprise and shock.

"Foul!" cried Marie, jumping to her feet.

"Sit down, my lady," said the cardinal. "There are no fouls in a trial by combat. Those men are not striving to see who is the better jouster, but to determine whose side God is on." Thibaut giggled and clapped.

Where was Valdemar? It was that thought that whirled through Falcon's mind as he struggled to control his mount. If he could not see the man, he must be behind him—an intolerable situation. He leaned low along the horse's neck and dug in the spurs. The mount leaped forward, and not an instant too soon, for just as he did, Falcon heard through his muffling coif the whistle of Valdemar's beheading stroke coming from behind and to the right.

As Falcon rode forward, Valdemar, a cunning warrior, stuck close to his foe's horse's right buttock. He had gained the ideal position in a fight between horsemen; by attacking from the right rear, his foe had to take his blows on the unshielded side, while being reduced to dealing backhand strokes against the pursuer's shield. Falcon knew this quite well. His backhand was powerful, but it was futile against Valdemar's heavy shield. He turned his steed one way and then another in a series of evasive maneuvers, but Valdemar's well-trained mount stuck like a burr.

There was one trick left. It depended on timing and whether his horse would still be perfectly responsive after being kicked in the mouth. It might not be able to feel the bit very well. No help for it. Falcon sank in his spurs and at the same instant, slipped his arm from the shield straps. He let the shield fall free and transferred his reins to his teeth. Grasping Moorslayer's hilt in both hands, he leaned back hard, jerking on the reins. The destrier sat back on its haunches as Falcon whirled Moorslayer in a tremendous arc that flashed horizontally from left to right with all the weight and power of Falcon's body behind it. Valdemar's own stroke, aimed at where Falcon was supposed to be, hissed by harmlessly. As Moorslayer met Valdemar's shield, it had not only Falcon's strength behind it, but the full momentum of the German's charge. The thick shield of iron and leather and wood smashed inward as if it were parchment, spraying Valdemar's face with splinters and sending him reeling in the saddle. As the German rode past, still miraculously mounted, Falcon soothed the stinging ache in his palms and tried to get his breath. Mortal combat is the most tiring experience in the world, and his breath was coming in ragged gasps that strove to fill his burning lungs. Then, whirling Moorslayer high, he set spurs and charged after the German.

Valdemar sat his horse, seemingly dazed. He held Helm-Cleaver loosely and swayed in the saddle, as if unaware that Falcon was thundering down upon him with Moorslayer raised high and slanting down his back for a blow that would hack the German from helm to crotch, and the crowd held its collective breath, about to witness the climax of the incredible combat.

Valdemar's daze was a ruse. As Moorslayer began to descend, the German spurred his mount into a short jump forward and released his sword to let it dangle from its retaining thong. As Moorslayer swung past, Valdemar gripped Falcon's wrist with one hand and thrust his other into the narrow space between Falcon's crotch and his saddle. With an immense heave of his huge body, aided by the momentum of Falcon's downward blow, Valdemar hoisted his enemy from his saddle and pitched him clear across his own horse and onto the ground beyond.

The roar that greeted this move dwarfed everything that had gone before. People were frantically jumping about, laughing and pounding on one another's backs, passing wineskins from hand to hand. Songs would grow from this battle, and they would be repeated for a hundred years.

Falcon heard none of it; nothing but a ringing in his ears. He saw nothing except the spots that swam in front of his eyes, and he tried to brush them away. He was struggling to his knees when a hoof slammed into his side. He went rolling, but the sudden shock cleared his head and he quickly regained his feet to see Valdemar charging down on him, mustaches aflutter. Where was Moorslayer? As the sword came down, Falcon dived forward and rolled, avoiding the blade by an inch. Frantically, he looked for Moorslayer. Then Valdemar was upon him again and Helm-Cleaver glanced from Falcon's fine Saracen helmet. The German thundered past, and Falcon knew he had to do something or he was lost.

Valdemar readied his last charge. It had been a splendid fight, simply wonderful. Never had he faced such a foe, but it was time to end it. He would prefer giving Falcon a slow death, but the man had given him too many surprises in this battle. Best to take no more chances. He would simply ride him down, trample him awhile, then dismount to whack his head off when he was safely unconscious. He leaned out to inspect his horse's spiked, iron-plated hoofs. All seemed in order. With a guttural yell, he charged. Falcon's reeling body was before him. Another instant and he would be atop him. Then, with incredible adroitness, Falcon sidestepped. Valdemar cursed, sawing at his reins. Where had the bastard gone? Then he felt the weight of Falcon's body on the cantle of his saddle and felt the arm that went around his shoulders and saw the dagger come around to smash into the heavy mail over his breast. The blade failed to penetrate through the doubled mail reinforcement that protected his chest, but he knew that the next would slide between coif and chin and into his throat. Only one thing left to do. Valdemar kicked his feet free of the stirrups and flung himself backward with all his weight.

They struggled, each wanting to land on top. They alit instead on their right sides and rolled apart. The cheering was continuous now, but the two men had no thought except to kill, to end this seemingly endless battle. Valdemar fought to untwist the thong that bound Helm-Cleaver to his wrist while Falcon ran to where he now saw Moorslayer lying in the grass. He snatched the sword from the ground and checked the grip to make sure that it had picked up no moisture from the grass. Gripping the hilt tightly in both fists, he strode slowly over to Valdemar. There was no hurry now, and he needed to regain his wind. The German awaited him, sword held likewise in both hands.

Valdemar swung Helm-Cleaver horizontally in a blow aimed to halve Falcon at the waist. Falcon blocked the blow with Moorslayer's flat. When two great swords, no matter how well forged, met edge to edge, both would be notched and perhaps broken. As the German's blade slid free, Falcon brought his own up, around, and down vertically. Valdemar went to one knee, grasping Helm-Cleaver at the grip in one hand and near the tip in the other, raising it above his head to intercept Moorslayer on the flat.

The German's arms bent outward like springs in absorbing the terrific shock, and Moorslayer clanged into his helmet, sending him to the ground. Falcon trod on Valdemar's sword arm and raised Moorslayer for the killing blow. In his red rage, he did not hear the shouts of dismay from the crowd. As Moorslayer was about to begin its fatal descent, Falcon felt something grip his wrists, then he was yanked backward to fall sprawling on his back. He was conscious of a pounding of hoofs, and of swirling white robes. He struggled to sit, and he saw two men in white Saracen robes and turbans mounted on small mares. One jumped to the ground and struggled to get Valdemar to his feet. The other was shouting in Arabic and recoiling the whip with which he'd foiled Falcon's killing blow. Then Valdemar was on a mare and the Saracen mounted behind him. The two horses sped for the crowd, the whip man popping his lash and clearing a space, but several onlookers were too slow and were trampled in consequence.

Falcon staggered to his feet, roaring and all but weeping in frustration. It had been so close! Then his men were around him, whooping and laughing, and he was borne on their shoulders to the dais.

Falcon was a ghastly sight, unhelmed now and with the coif thrown back to show that he was bleeding from both ears. Blood had gushed from his nose and spread all over the breast of his mailshirt, but Marie thought him the most beautiful sight she had ever seen.

Cardinal Eusebius stood and signaled for silence. This time, it was several minutes before he got it. "The decision of God has been clear in this matter. The Lady Marie de Cleves is innocent of all wrongdoing. The Baron Thibaut de Cleves is guilty of the foul sin of seizing the land of men on Crusade. As soon as the rites may be performed, he shall be declared excommunicate and condemned by bell, book, and candle. He shall henceforth be denied fire, water, food, and shelter by all communicants of Holy Mother Church until it shall please the Holy Father that he has performed sufficient penance to merit being received among Christians again." The crowd cheered wildly, and Thibaut writhed in an agony of fear and mortification.

"As for the former Sir Gunther Valdemar," Eusebius went on, when he had quiet once more, "he is hereby declared a false and recreant knight and is hereby declared degraded from the degree of honorable knighthood. When he is again seen among Christians, any knight may hale him into a public place, there to have his sword broken before him by the public executioner, and his gilded spurs hacked from his heels by a nightsoil collector. With broken sword and spurs tied about his neck, he is to be seated upon an ass, with his face to its rump, and driven from the town." The public uproar thundered out again. The knight Ruy Ortiz held his sword Moorslayer once more, kissing the blade that had won new honors.

"As for you, young man," said the cardinal to Falcon, in a lower voice, "if you were a better Christian, you'd be a credit to the institution of knighthood." Then the mob was off, to carry their new hero throughout the delirious city.

SEVEN

WULF poured the wine. Falcon had been abed for two days now, recovering from the terrible battering he had taken at the hands of Gunther Valdemar. Incredibly, he had suffered no serious fractures. His body, however, was a solid mass of black and blue, bruised in every part by the blows and falls of the combat. It was a drawback of mail armor that while it kept cutting edges and piercing points from the wearer's flesh, it did nothing to absorb the shock of blows.

To make matters worse, the burns his feet had received on the night of Valdemar's attack were festering, causing him even greater agony. He did not cry out, but Wulf could see from the paleness of his face and the set of his jaw what his master and friend was going through. He handed the cup to Falcon, and it was taken with a slightly trembling hand.

Falcon drank the crimson liquid gratefully, feeling its cheer spread through his limbs and dulling the pain a little. Even holding the cup was a strain. The tremendous backhand blow that had smashed Valdemar's shield had wrenched Falcon's elbows cruelly. He lay back with a sigh against the pillows.

"Does that help, my lord?" Wulf asked. They were alone. Marie had been with Draco all morning, but she had had to leave to attend to the business of the castle.

"A little," Falcon replied. "Christ Jesus, but I've been hurt worse than this and not taken so long to recover!"

"Shall I mix a bit of the poppy gum with the wine?" Wulf asked.

"I'd rather save that for the fevers. You know it brings on the dreams."

"Aye, but it also brings on sleep. You've not slept for three nights, and unless you do, your hurts will never heal. Who knows what Valdemar is doing? He may be escaping this minute and you lying here unable to pursue."

"No, he'll not run. He won't want to leave me alive behind his back. You're right, though. I can't stay here uselessly while the bastard plots. Mix me a sleeping potion."

Wulf went to the pouch that sat upon the chest in the corner. From it he took a lump of the poppy gum and broke off a piece. He smashed the piece as always and poured the red wine over it, mixing it with a large, blunt finger. He handed the cup to Falcon, and his master drank, wincing slightly at the bitter taste. Then he lay back on the pillows. His eyelids grew heavy, and his breathing became deep and regular. He was asleep.

Wulf left the chamber and closed the door. The dark, cavelike castle corridor was illuminated only by a smoky rushlight set in a sconce. Wulf seated himself in the dank straw on the floor with his back against the door and laid his falchion across his knees. While his master was in his drugged sleep, nobody, not even Marie de Cleves, would be permitted to enter and perhaps hear what Draco might cry out in his dreams. Wulf passed the time in listening to the water drip from the walls and the rats rustling about in the straw.

Within the chamber, Falcon was sinking deeper into sleep, and deeper into his past. His nostrils twitched. They did not react to the damp smells of the castle. They stung with the dust and hot winds of Outremer.

Draco de Montfalcon stood on the parapet of the castle, stroking the beautiful gyrfalcon. In Europe, the lordly gyr could be flown only by a king, and Draco's position as a mere squire would have decreed that he fly a lanneret. His father, as an earl, could fly the splendid peregrine. But here in Outremer, almost any man of rank could fly the gyr if he wished. Draco carefully placed the bird in its mews and examined the cage minutely to be sure that it was clean. It always was. The falconers knew better than to be slack about their bird-keeping. European castles were often veritable sties for filth, but the mews would be spotless.

He took the roof-stair down into the great hall. In contrast to the cramped, dark castles he had been accustomed to at home, the new castles of Outremer were large and spacious. The walls were hung with huge Persian tapestries, and open spaces in the roof let in the light, for rain was so rare that it need not even be considered.

Seated at the table in the great hall with winecups before them were his father, Eudes de Montfalcon, and his four inseparable companions—the Englishman Nigel Edgehill, the German Gunther Valdemar, the Flemish Archbishop de Beaumont, and his boyhood friend from home, Odo FitzRoy. They looked up as Draco entered and beckoned to him, smiling.

"Come join us, Draco, my lad," called de Beaumont. The archbishop was a jolly, rubicund man whose rolls of fat sheathed a frame of iron. He rode into battle at the head of his men with his clerical robe over his armor and a huge wooden cudgel in his fist, for he was forbidden by his holy orders to "smile with the edge of the sword."

"Draco the Lightning-Proof," laughed Edgehill. Edgehill was a short redheaded man whose father was lord of the manor of Edgehill in Warwickshire, granted to his great-grandfather by William the Conqueror for services at Hastings and in the later conquest of England. Draco winced slightly at the nickname, for he hated to be reminded of the terrible night at sea.

"Have a cup with us, young Draco," grunted Valdemar. Of all his father's friends, Draco liked Valdemar the least. The man was an ape masquerading as a gentleman. He saw that FitzRoy was rolling up some parchments with an oddly suspicious haste. What had they been discussing?

"Yes, join us, my son," Eudes said. He looked strangely disturbed. If Draco had not known his father better, he would have thought that he looked frightened. But that was impossible. Whatever the cause, he seemed grateful for Draco's interruption. Draco took the cup that de Beaumont handed him and sat at the table.

"We've just been discussing . . ." Edgehill seemed to grope for words. "Well, your coming knighthood."

"Yes," Odo broke in, as if to cover for Edgehill's fumbling words, "Guy of Lusignan has agreed to give you the accolade himself."

"The king!" Draco's suspicions were swept away by elation. Guy of Lusignan was king of the fantastic Crusader Kingdom of Jerusalem.

"And Raymond of Tripoli will stand as your sponsor," said Valdemar. Raymond was the Prince of Galilee! The honor was little short of overwhelming.

"I shall belt on your sword myself," said Odo, "and Nigel will give you your spurs." Odo FitzRoy was a tall, strikingly handsome man with aquiline features and black hair just beginning to go gray at the temples. He was one of the best axe fighters in the army, and his unscarred face and faultless teeth attested to his skillful management of his shield. He was the only one of his father's friends that Draco truly liked and respected. He had been "Uncle Odo" for as long as Draco could remember and had taken responsibility for much of Draco's training, especially in norsemanship. It had been in Odo's castle of Quinon that Draco had been put through his early squireship.

"When will the ceremony be?" Draco asked eagerly.

"Very soon," Odo said. "As soon as we've settled this trouble with Malik en Nasr." That was puzzling. Odo referred to the sultan who had at last unified the Moslems of Outremer and declared the holy war upon the Crusader kingdoms, but he referred to him by his Arabic title instead of by the corruption of his name by which he was usually known to the Crusaders; Saladin.

"One last battle should decide the matter," de Beaumont said. Four of the men smiled at each other, but Eudes de Montfalcon wore a distressed frown. Valdemar rose from where he was sitting.

"Let's adjourn to my castle at Hattin," the German said. "My huntsmen have spotted a lion in the hills and I'm in need of some sport."

"A lion!" Eudes said. Draco's father was passionately fond of hunting, his one enthusiasm not shared by his son. Draco was fond of game, but never hunted for sport. "What do you say to that, Draco? Shall we go?"

Draco was about to assent when de Beaumont broke in smoothly. "I fear we'll have to forgo young Draco's company. The constable is holding an inspection of all the warhorses this afternoon, and all the squires must attend with their mounts and their lords'."

Draco cursed silently. He'd forgotten.

"Well, come along tomorrow then, Draco," Eudes said. The five men left, Eudes still wearing his look of uncertainty. Once he seemed about to turn back, but Odo took his arm and led him through the door. Draco looked after them with an unsettled heart.

When the inspection was over, Draco took his mount back to the stable, leading his father's great destrier by his right hand. His own horse he turned over to Wulf, the other to his father's handler, a Saracen named Ayub.

"Will your father be riding out in the morning, young master?" asked Ayub. He was a man of about thirty, with a thin face and a pointed beard.

"No, I'll be exercising him myself, Ayub," Draco answered. "Father's gone to Hattin to hunt."

"Ah, Hattin. That is my village. Does he hunt antelope?"

"No, Valdemar's huntsmen found a lion."

The Saracen looked puzzled. "But young master, there have been no lions near Hattin for a hundred years!"

At the words, Draco's face went white. His earlier suspicions came crowding back. "Wulf, Ayub, saddle the swiftest coursers in the stable. We ride for Hattin!"

Through the thick wood of the castle door, Wulf could hear Falcon's drugged muttering. Then there was a shout: "Father! Father!" Then silence for a while, then: "Odo! I'll drink your blood!"

Wulf sighed and leaned back against the door, fondling the hilt of the falchion across his knees. He knew what would come next.

Valdemar's castle of Hattin was little more than a hill-fort across the valley from the pointed rock formation called the Horns of Hattin. It was like a hundred other border outposts established to protect the Crusader kingdoms from Saracen incursions.

The three men dismounted well below the castle, visible now only as a jagged shadow against the starry sky. They scrambled up the rocky slope. At the base of the castle wall Ayub took the small grappling hook from his belt and shook out its rope. He whirled it around a few times and cast it up the wall to the battlement. It dropped into a crenel and clinked against the stone beyond. They held their breaths for a few seconds, waiting for an alarm to be raised at the sound. All was silence. Slowly, Ayub drew in on the rope, and the hook dragged across the stone walk, then up the low wall. Then the points wedged firmly against the edge of the crenel and its flanking merlon. Ayub gave it a few tugs to seat the hook solidly, then he handed the rope to Draco. As the strongest, Draco was obliged to go first.

Greatsword slung across his back, Draco gripped the rope and began to pull himself up. Hard-callused as his hands were, the rope bit painfully. He was beyond pain this night, though. Slowly, a foot at a time, he dragged himself up to the battlement and through the notch of the crenel. He scrambled across until he was standing on the wallwalk. He crouched there, listening for sentries. There were none. That was odd, but it was in his favor. He could hear sounds from the courtyard below, but they were distant enough not to be threatening.

Ayub and then Wulf came scrambling up the rope, with Draco's assistance. He signalled that they were to descend into the courtyard by the steps nearest the keep. As they padded along the wallwalk, hugging the battlement, they saw what was going on in the courtyard below. There was a small campfire burning, and around it were seated about twenty men in white desert robes and turbans. Had the place been taken by the Saracens? Draco feared far worse.

Staying in the shadow, they crossed to the keep and crept along the wall toward the door. To Draco's immense relief, it stood open. They entered. The ground floor was a warren of narrow passages, and Draco was at a loss where to go. The place seemed deserted, so whatever the business at hand, his father's friends wanted no witnesses. Then he heard the screams.

Wulf's hand clamped on his shoulder as Draco surged forward. The scream was unmistakably in his father's voice. "Give us away now and we're all dead, master, and no help to our lord." In the dim rushlight, he could see

Ayub nodding vigorously. He strove to calm his growing rage and padded softly toward the hideous noises.

A lurid glare flickered up a stairway carved deep in the rock beneath the castle. Draco slid his sword silently from its sheath, and his two companions likewise drew their weapons—Wulf a short sword and Ayub a scimitar. They tiptoed down the last steps and came to an open door. Inside was a sight that nearly drove the remnants of sanity from Draco's mind. Eudes de Montfalcon lay strapped down to a table, his body a mass of smoking, ragged flesh drenched in blood. Over him stood a hulking Saracen who held a glowing iron. Around the table were ranged his four "friends," de Beaumont, Edgehill, Valdemar, and FitzRoy. To one side stood a tall, dignified Saracen in a plain robe. A fold of his cloak was drawn across the Saracen's face.

"Tell us!" cried FitzRoy. "You must tell us! I am your friend, Eudes. I offered you everything. You could have been a great one if you'd joined us. Tell us what we need to know and you still may!"

There was nothing from the man on the table but a deep groan. De Beaumont nodded to the torturer. The iron came down again.

"My time is short," the Saracen said. "You must work more quickly!"

With a strangled scream, Draco was in the room and charging for the table. Instantly he was blocked by a line of Saracen swordsmen. The amir had brought his bodyguard. A swipe of Draco's sword whipped the guts from one, and the return blow took off a head. More took their place.

"Run, Draco, save yourself!" It was his father's voice. "Warn—" He was silenced by a blow from FitzRoy. Draco was pressed back up the stair along with his companions and at the top swung the door shut, catching and breaking a scimitar-waving arm in the process. There was no way to bolt the door from this side, so the three ran for the main entrance. Behind them, they could hear the sounds of the pursuit. Bursting through the main door, they swung it on its massive hinges, but, like all other doors in any castle, there was no way to bar it from opening outward. They ran into the courtyard, where men were stirring from the fire, taking up arms at the sounds of alarm.

Draco saw a small force scurry to guard the castle gate. No way out there, then. "To the wall," he said to his companions. They made a dash for the nearest stairway leading from the courtyard to the wallwalk. A group of men tried to cut them off. Draco ducked beneath the slash of a scimitar and gutted the man who wielded it. He saw Ayub cut down by a pack of Saracens, who continued to slash at the inert body long after it was dead. Draco and Wulf broke loose.

At the base of the stair, Draco's way was suddenly blocked by a huge figure in a desert burnous over Frankish armor. "Try me, pretty boy," said the man in French. "By God's whiskers. I'll have your—" At that moment, Draco took a mighty swing at the veiled head. The man blocked easily with the flat of his greatsword and sent back a blow that Draco blocked imperfectly. The flat of his own sword was driven back against his head and he was knocked sprawling. The man bestrode him, sword upraised for the killing stroke. Then the Saxon horseboy, Wulf, was bestriding him, thin legs stretched wide to span Draco's big body, and the lad was taking on the big Frank, who had three times his bulk.

The big man was nonplussed for an instant, then: "Out of the way, you common filth!" He tried to brush the boy aside, but the short sword flashed, and with a surprised curse the man jumped back with a badly slashed forearm. Draco scrambled to his feet and the two young men hot-footed it up the stair, closely pursued by the Saracens.

They arrived at the spot where they had mounted the wall. To Draco's relief, the grapple was still in place.

"You go first," Wulf gasped, "I'll hold—" Draco grasped the boy by the scruff of the neck and flung him into the crenel, then planted his feet and faced his enemies. A white-robed form thrust forward with a spear, and Draco sidestepped and brought the greatsword down, cleaving the man to the waist. For the first time this night, he felt he was behaving as a knight should, as he had trained to act. His rage and frustration were immense, and drove him to feats of ferocity that had the Saracens tumbling back over one another in ragged retreat. *I should not be here!* he thought. *I should be back down there with him!* He almost tripped over a head that lay among the limbs and piles of entrails with which his sword had littered the wallwalk. Then the way was clear and he rushed back to the crenel.

" 'Ware the blade!" Draco shouted, and he dropped the greatsword down the wall. Swinging his body over the edge, he slid down the rope, ignoring the agony in his palms. Above him, a Saracen sawed at the rope, and it parted. Draco's heart leaped into his mouth, then his feet hit the ground, no more than two feet below.

Wulf thrust the sword into his hand, grabbed his shoulder, and propelled him down the hill to where the horses were tethered. As they mounted, Draco gasped out: "I should have killed him, Wulf! I should have killed him!"

"Which one, master? They all need killing," Wulf said.

"Father! I should have not left him there alive!"

"He's dead now for sure, master. You saw what they did to him. Let's ride. His death should not be wasted. We must warn King Guy!"

But as they rode away, Draco's mind whirled. Warn him of what? What incredible treachery was afoot back there? The two horses pounded away into the Outremer night.

Wulf looked up. He had slept with his back against the door and his neck was stiff. A swish of fragrant skirts had wakened him. Lady Marie was standing before him. He got creakily to his feet.

"Good morning, my lady."

"It's afternoon, Wulf. How is Draco?"

Wulf cocked an ear to the door and heard nothing.

"Sleeping, my lady. Best we don't disturb him."

"I'd like to see him anyway." She tried to open the door but Wulf thrust an arm across it.

"While my lord is not himself, no one may enter, my lady. I am sorry."

Marie flushed. "I will see him!"

"No, my lady," Wulf said, not unkindly.

"You base lout! Stand aside!" She slapped Wulf across the face twice. He weathered the weak blows with no change of expression. "I am sorry, my lady."

Suddenly, Marie broke into sobs. "Forgive me, Wulf. I know you are his friend. It makes me jealous that you are something to him that I can never be. It is just that I worry so about him when he is hurt like this. Forgive me."

"Nothing to forgive, my lady. I've slain men who stood between me and my Lord Draco. But when he is like this he is not in his right mind. Sometimes he says things that no one should hear. Not even you."

"I know that Draco has had a tortured past. Sometimes . . ." she blushed, but then went on, "Sometimes, in his sleep, he cries out names, things that mean nothing to me. Hattin, and FitzRoy, and Beaumont. Hattin, of course, the whole world knows about. But is the rest so terrible?"

"It is something the world had best not know about, my lady. I tell you this much only because you have become closer to my lord than any since his father's death, but Lord Draco knows things that could near destroy Christendom; things that, were they generally known, would bring down the kingdoms of Outremer, even destroy the Throne of St. Peter."

Marie gasped. "What happened over there in Outremer? I never suspected! I knew that Draco thirsted for revenge, and that it was something about the treacherous death of his father, but I never dreamed . . ."

"He lives for that revenge, my lady. For the rest, he cares nothing. Whether the papacy falls tomorrow or lasts another thousand years he cares not a whit. But there are four men whose every breath is an affront to him. They must die, my lady. We have both pledged our lives to that, as once we pledged them to preserving the Holy Sepulcher. But if it were known that Draco has the knowledge that is in his head this moment, then whole armies would be dispatched to hunt him down and slay him. No one must know." He settled his back against the door. "I have already said too much, my lady, but I thought I owed you no less."

"I am grateful for your confidence, Wulf. I know that what is between you and Draco is far more than what ordinarily passes between master and man. You are his friend. I am glad that you wish to be my friend, too."

"I would be less than your friend, my lady, if I did not warn you that you will not be able to hold Lord Draco. He will never rest until justice has been served at sword's point to four men. It may take his whole life, and he may have to comb the whole of Christendom, and beyond."

Marie's head sagged. These were the words she had most feared to hear. Then her chin rose. "If that is his path, then so be it. I know what it is to love a father, and to sacrifice everything else for him. When it is time for him to go, I shall not stay him. But I do wish to see him. Please call me, Wulf, when he is himself again."

Wulf bowed and she had turned to go when a voice rang out through the thick door: "Wulf! What's all that clamor out there? If that's my little wench, show her in. I'm wasting away from loneliness in here!"

With a glad cry, Marie brushed past Wulf and hauled the door open. She dashed across the room and threw herself into Draco's arms. The breath went out of him in a whoosh, but he wrapped his arms about her and rocked her small body back and forth on the bed while Wulf discreetly closed the door and went to pour cups of wine. Without asking permission, he poured one for himself. He took two of the cups and gave them to the happy couple on the bed.

Draco smiled as he tipped his cup to his lips. "Take a look at my feet, Wulf." Obediently, Wulf bent and drew back the cover. He unwrapped the bandage and examined the burns. There was no more seepage of pus, and the yellowed peelings of old skin were curling back like parchment to reveal new, pink skin growing beneath.

"Healing cleanly, my lord," Wulf reported.

"Good. Maybe I'll try trial by fire next time." He chuckled as Marie slapped him across the chest, then stopped as the laughter pained his damaged ribs.

"Where are they, Wulf?" Falcon asked.

The Saxon looked at his master, then at Marie.

"They're holed up at Thibaut's castle, my lord."

"And what are they doing?"

"They wait," Marie said. "They dare not attack now, with the *pacata* still at hand. You can be sure the barons roundabout are plotting a storm of Pierre Noir, now that Thibaut is excommunicate."

"Then we'll have to attack first," Falcon said.

"When you're fully healed," Marie protested.

"That may be too late. When I accepted your service, Marie, I undertook to destroy this Thibaut and win the gold you need to ransom your father. This I will do, sick or well." Marie had to shrink from the power of his eyes.

There was something here that was beyond her experience.

"As you will, Draco," she said. "But I need only the five hundred ducats. I would not have you risk yourself for more."

"Thibaut and the five hundred ducats I will deliver into your hands, my lady," Falcon said. "But Valdemar I must have for myself."

In the following days, training and drilling went on at a furious pace. The emphasis now was on castle sieging instead of open battle in the field. In contrast to the usual haphazard method of laying a siege, Falcon insisted on a methodical, systematic approach.

With a small party that included his engineer, Rupert Foul-Mouth, Falcon rode out on a reconnaissance of the castle of Pierre Noir. With charcoal and parchment, he made notes, and he took a few prisoners—workmen from the castle who could provide information about its defenses. Thibaut was not a beloved master, so it was not even necessary to torture the prisoners.

In the bailey at La Roche, Falcon had a model of the hill and castle of Pierre Noir constructed. The model was accurate to the smallest detail, with twigs representing the nearby trees placed in their proper locations. With this model, Falcon and Rupert explained the operation repeatedly, until every man knew his part.

Rupert distrusted Falcon's written notes, entirely uncertain that the strange, scratchy little lines could contain the solid realities of stone and earth and wood. With the model, though, he was delighted, and he strode around it like a schoolmaster, pointing with a sword to the various items as he reeled them off.

"Now here," Rupert said, indicating a series of wooden galleries built over the top of the stone wall, "he's built him some hoardings. Them's wood and will burn right merrily, but watch your crusty arses, because he's been collecting oil and pitch enough to start his own little hell. Now here—" he pointed to some elaborate battlements built to hang out over the face of the wall—" he's constructing some of them fucking new-fangled machicolations.

"Lord Shitface over there keeps adding new defenses to this dungheap because he's hose-messing scared of his neighbors, and well he might be. Three corners of the outer wall have the new round towers that are hard to sap, but the southeast corner is still square, and that's what we'll try to break down first. We go in under wheeled sheds and ram away at that corner like a friar going at a ewe. She'll come down and we're in slick as shit on the doorsill."

The inner keep was another matter. It was a tall round tower with a steep roof sheathed in lead, a far cry from the antiquated design of La Roche.

"Short of demolishing the outer wall," Falcon said while Rupert rested from his labors and took a nip of wine, "we'll not be able to bring siege engines to bear against the keep. We'll have to try storming it or starving them out." Both were grim prospects. Storming a castle always resulted in heavy losses for the attackers, and the filth and crowding of a siege camp inevitably led to pestilence. More often than not, a siege had to be lifted because the attacking force fell too far below strength through the attrition of sickness. "We can't tunnel under it." Falcon continued, "because it's built on solid rock. A ram won't pierce that wall, and the main gate has a double portcullis." It was a daunting prospect.

"You may leave the next step to me," Falcon said. "I have a plan. If it works, we'll be in without taking too many losses. For now, let's concentrate on breaching the outer wall. I'll take you through the whole process again." The men groaned and, for the fiftieth time, had their roles explained to them.

To avoid the delay of cutting timber to build his siege works at the site, Falcon had all the sheds, wagons, towers, ladders, and catapults built at La Roche, then disassembled to be transported by wagon and cart to Pierre Noir. It was necessary to lay in ample supplies of food for the men and fodder for the animals, since Thibaut was sure to have picked his district clean in anticipation of a long siege.

There was always the likelihood of foul weather, so Falcon made sure that there were plenty of waterproof tents and even insisted on lumber to build wooden barracks should the siege prove a long one. Wagons covered with canvas held dry firewood should none be available.

When all was in readiness, they marched on Pierre Noir.

EIGHT

THE watchman atop the keep scanned the fields surrounding Pierre Noir. The early-morning mist was beginning to disperse, and the song of birds made the day pleasant. The fields looked bare and featureless, because every trace of tree and brush had been cut back to a distance of a thousand paces to provide no cover for an enemy. The gleaming, whitewashed splendor of Pierre Noir stood from the black rock for which it was named like a solid feature of the landscape, foreboding, enduring, and unshakable. The banners waved lazily in the faint breeze that had sprung up. The breeze carried with it sounds that were foreign to the district and the fine morning—the creak of ungreased wooden wheels, the bellowing of many oxen, the hoofbeats of horses, the clink of armed men.

"Host approaching!" the watchman shouted down to the men in the bailey below.

Thibaut looked up at the shout. Valdemar, armored as usual, snorted. "About time."

"Will they try to storm us immediately?" Thibaut fretted. "Perhaps we should get into the keep and wall up the door."

"We've plenty of time," Valdemar said disgustedly. "It takes days to set up a siege properly. But by all means go to the keep if you want. I'll be at my proper place on the outer wall. I won't take to the keep until that falls. Just don't you shut the door behind me and my men, or I'll join forces with Draco and kill you myself." Huge in his bulky hauberk, the German strode for the wall. After a moment's hesitation, Thibaut hobbled after him.

From the top of the outer wall, they could see the force from La Roche setting up camp. The work was progressing swiftly, with tents and sheds going up just beyond bowshot from the wall.

"There are a lot of them." Thibaut said, wringing his hands.

"Falcon's own force is no more than fifty," Valdemar said, making a rough count. "Maybe twice that many more will be volunteers who want to defend La Roche and have the pleasure of putting you over a slow fire."

Thibaut closed his eyes and tried to swallow, but his throat was dry. The prospect of suffering as he had made so many suffer was not pleasant.

"Cheer up, my lord." Valdemar said jovially, slapping Thibaut on the hump. "It'll be good practice for Hell. And that's where you'll go for dying excommunicate!" The German slapped his thigh and roared while Thibaut turned pale at his brutal humor.

Wiping the tears of laughter from his eyes, Valdemar turned serious again. "I may have misinformed you, Thibaut," he said.

"Misinformed me how?"

"Those bastards aren't going to need days to get ready. They'll attack tomorrow morning."

"How can that be?" Thibaut demanded, scanning the opposing force with dread.

"See, they've brought all their gear with them ready-made." The German pointed to where tall poles were being lashed together into a framework. "That's a siege tower going up there. And there are catapults being erected, too. That Draco is a knight of Outremer, there's no denying it. Most of your neighbors would still be fighting over who got the best tentsite."

In the opposing camp, where the cookfires were already alight, Falcon and Wulf stood examining the gate before them. Around them stood a knot of the underofficers: Guido, who commanded the archers, Donal, who had charge of the foot soldiers, Ruy Ortiz, commander of the horsemen, and Rupert Foul-Mouth, the engineer.

"There the bastards are," Falcon said, pointing to the group of men atop the gate. "Both of them. Guido, what are the chances of getting them both right now with bolts or arrows?"

The Italian judged the range by eye and examined the way the wind flapped the banners atop the castle towers. "No good, my lord. The range is just a little too long and the wind is wrong."

"Pity," Falcon said.

"But my lord," Ruy protested, "you've not yet made your challenge to them." The Spanish knight took the newly developing rules of chivalry very seriously, and his master's callousness sometimes disturbed him.

"I have no use for such fripperies," Falcon said, "and you can be sure that Valdemar has none. If it would win me a siege without the loss of a man, I'd send in an assassin to put poison in their cups." Scandalized, the Spanish knight kept his silence.

"Look at them toad-fuckers," said Rupert. "They think they're safe as pigs in shit. Well, wait'll my lads have at that goat-pronging gate. They'll be through it quick as an abbess doing the new novice with the Easter candle." They all howled with laughter except for Ortiz, who could hack a man in two without turning a hair but who blushed at foul language.

"Ruy, you should have been a Hospitaler!" Falcon said, when he had breath to speak.

"I have considered joining the Temple," Ortiz said, primly.

Falcon sobered. "Stay away from the Templars, Ruy. They're not what they seem. After Hattin . . ." Wulf took Falcon's arm and silenced him with a warning glance. The others seemed not to have noticed, and Falcon shrugged his arm free. "Well, if you must, join the Hospitalers. They're better fighters, and the Temple's too rich." He turned his attention to the frantic activity all around him.

As a result of Falcon's endless rehearsals, the siege camp and machinery were going up with unusual speed. Everywhere Falcon's soldiers labored alongside the La Roche volunteers and work gangs of drafted peasants. In other armies, men did not don armor until just before a battle. Now, in the field, Falcon's men wore armor even on work details.

Because there had been a shortage of good rope in the district, it had been impossible for Rupert to construct torsion catapults, the kind using twisted rope for power. Instead, he had built trebuchets—towering stone-throwers that used a falling weight for motive force. A trebuchet consisted of a tall supporting framework holding a stout crossbar. Pivoted to the crossbar was a long throwing arm. The longer limb of the arm ended in a sling. The shorter end had a huge box full of stones and earth. When the sling end was cranked back to the ground and the sling loaded, the weight box was raised. When the sling was released, the weight came down, the mast whipped up, and the missile hurtled on a high trajectory at the enemy fortification.

The trebuchet was the most powerful of all catapults. A big one could cast a dead horse for six hundred yards into an enemy city. The same could be done with live prisoners. Sometimes the monotony of a long siege would be relieved by sending in humorous loads, such as sacks

123

of enemy heads, hornet nests, or huge bags of human excrement.

One work gang was constructing a wheeled shed. It was a wooden framework roofed with wet hides. Hung from the roofbeam was a ram—a log tipped with iron. Inside it in action would be oxen for motive power and men to swing the ram.

The siege towers were on wheels, too. Built to overtop the outer wall, they were wood-sheathed and covered with wet hides against fire. Their top platforms would hold armed men. A tower would be pushed by oxen against the enemy wall, the drawbridge atop the structure would fall, and the men would rush across it and onto the enemy battlement. More would rush up its stair to reinforce those on the wall and establish a foothold.

There were other machines—moles to drill holes in the walls, a tedious process; spankers, simple devices using the smacking impact of a bent, springy board to cast several javelins at once; tortoises, covered shelters to be placed against the base of a wall and allow workmen to mine away at it. Each had its function, and under their cumulative strength even the finest castle could be brought down in time. But time was the enemy, too.

Patience. Patience had not come easily to him, but he had learned. Two years pulling an oar in a stinking Turkish galley had taught him patience and self-discipline. Without them he would have died. But he had learned the true disciplines from Suleiman the Wise. The old man's face came before his mind's eye, and the intervening years faded to nothing.

"Draco, my son," Suleiman said, stroking his graying beard, "you have all the makings of a great man save that of self-discipline. In your rage you have great strength, and I believe this to be a blessing from Allah, but it does you little good if you cannot bring it under control." Falcon, now a grown man, his back covered with stripes from Abu's whip and his mind fixed in a mold of bitterness, shifted nervously on the cushion where he sat cross-legged. He didn't know where all this was leading.

"Even now," Suleiman continued, "you twitch like a schoolboy learning his first letters, you who sat at the oar bench with such exemplary patience."

"I was chained," Falcon muttered.

Suleiman glared at him. "You wear no chains here. I do not force you to learn. You are free to go, as you have been since I took you and your friends from the galley." Falcon flinched, his face flushed with shame. For all the horrors of his boyhood and young manhood—the lighting, the Crusade, the betrayal and death of his father, the galley, experiences which should have turned his feelings to stone—he still quailed before Suleiman's displeasure. This was not because he feared the old man, but because he loved and respected Suleiman more than any man since his father.

"I'm sorry, master," Falcon said, bowing deeply. "Please teach me what I must know."

"That's better," Suleiman said. "Abraham tells me that you are learning letters remarkably well for one who has come to study them so late in life. That pleases me, even though I know that your main purpose in learning is that you hope that such knowledge will help you to track down and slay your father's betrayers." The old man paused, considering his next words. "I cannot find any real fault in this. It is a man's duty to avenge a kinsman, especially his father. I had to avenge my own when I was no older than you. Filial piety comes before all other obligations save obedience to the will of Allah. Still, I do not hold with those who say that vengeance is the first of the Three Great Joys. If you dedicate your life to vengeance, then you will have no purpose when your vengeance has been accomplished.

"Beginning today, young Draco, I will teach you the

mental and spiritual disciplines which you must command in order to control your rages. The learning will be long and hard, but when you are finished, you will be your own master. You will still be able to call upon your great strength at need, but you will be its master, not it yours." Suleiman gestured behind him, where, as always, his sword bearer held the great sword Three Moons. "I have said that one day Three Moons will be yours, but you will never bear her unless you are worthy."

That day began the most difficult lessons of Draco's young life. The toils of war were as nothing to the work of self-mastery, but he had learned, and now as he sat before a small castle unthinkably far from Suleiman's homeland, his hand rested upon the crescent pommel of the sword Nemesis, which had once been called Three Moons.

"Are your diggers ready, Rupert?" Falcon asked.

"Soon as it's dark, my lord, we'll go out and prepare your little surprise for you." The old engineer chuckled appreciatively. "By Job's left ball, but they'll look like the friar who found out he was pronging the—" A glare from Ruy Ortiz cut off the obscene simile, but the man went on chuckling.

For some time, men had been arriving on horseback. They were a mixed group; neighboring lords, idle knights, troubadors, and just plain gawkers, all come to watch the spectacle of the siege of Pierre Noir. Falcon didn't object, as long as they stayed out of the way. Their reports would spread, and the reputation of Draco Falcon and his company would begin to grow. Soon the whores and jesters would be arriving to service and amuse the men. If the siege lasted long enough, a regular market would be set up. Falcon would have to keep a tight rein on his men or things could easily get out of hand.

Falcon strode to where the newcomers were gathering and addressed them. "You are welcome if you are here as observers, but I must ask you to stay well behind the siege line and not disturb my men. I will not be responsible for anyone's safety. If any of you wish to join my forces against Thibaut, please see me in my tent this afternoon. The division of the spoil will be strict and I will allow no indiscriminate looting." There were scowls at this, and several villainous-looking men turned their horses and rode away. The troubadors were already tuning their harps and rehearsing the opening lines of the songs they were composing to commemorate the occasion. Ordinarily, a petty siege such as this would not have attracted so much attention, but the story of the trial by combat had spread far, and many wanted to see its conclusion.

Wulf led Draco's horse to him, and he mounted. With a final look at his siege works to make sure that all was going well, he spurred toward the castle gate, Wulf riding behind him bearing the white flag of truce. This was something Falcon could have done without, but with the *pacata* so close at hand, it was essential that the formalities be observed.

He halted below the walls and stared up at the group gathered above. "I am Draco Falcon!" he shouted. "And I call upon the excommunicate Thibaut de Cleves to engage me in single combat, to meet me army to army on the open field, or to endure my siege. I hereby give him my mortal defiance!" Tearing off his right gauntlet, he cast it to the ground.

There was a wait of a few minutes, then the sound of bars being drawn back. The castle gate creaked open and Valdemar, wearing a look of profound boredom, emerged. He stooped to pick up the gauntlet and recited his part of the ritual in a monotone: "I, Gunther Valdemar, on behalf of my liege, Thibaut de Cleves, do accept your defiance and cast it back at you, choosing the siege. I will hold the castle of Pierre Noir while there is breath in my body, and you may strive to take it as you will." He handed the spiked gauntlet back to Falcon and said in his ordinary voice: "I'd ram this up your arse, but I suspect that bugger Abu stretched it so you'd never even feel the spikes."

Falcon snarled like an enraged beast. "You'll die slowly, pig!" He whirled and rode for his lines. Valdemar smiled, turned, and slowly ambled back inside. The gate shut behind him.

That evening, Falcon watched as his workmen labored under cover of darkness. Men came back from the work bearing baskets of earth while others went forward with sharpened stakes. Satisfied that all was going well, Falcon returned to his tent. Inside it were a number of the men who had been observing earlier. Among them was a representative of Cardinal Eusebius.

The cardinal's man looked up as Falcon walked in. "My lord," he said, "you must remember that the cardinal will insist on the proper conduct of war between Christians."

"Why?" Falcon said. "Thibaut's not a Christian, he's an excommunicate."

"His men are not," the man pointed out.

"So? When the Pope puts a nation under interdict, anyone who dies in the interim is buried unshriven. People suffer for the faults of their rulers. It's the same everywhere, and I didn't make it that way.

"I'm a man of war. I fight and win the best way I know how. I will not conduct a battle to suit a churchman or his notions of how best to butcher Christians." There were many broad grins at this, for the whole area was a hotbed of schism, heresy, and anticlerical sentiment. It was a common saying in southern France that the whole Roman Church was filthy as Jeremiah's loincloth.

Falcon drank watered wine and talked wars and horses

with the knights present, while a troubador sang of Roland and the battle of Roncesvalles.

It was late at night when Falcon was roused from a half-sleep by the blast of a trumpet. Grabbing up shield and ax, Falcon rushed from the tent and climbed the low earthen wall thrown up around the camp. The field between camp and castle was dotted with torchlight. Valdemar was trying a nighttime sally to set fire to the siege engines. Falcon had been expecting just such a maneuver and awaited their discovery of his surprise.

There was a shout of alarm, then the approaching torches stopped amid sounds of confusion. The horses and men were falling into the system of trenches and pits Rupert's men had dug. There were shrieks as men were thrown from their horses to be impaled on the sharpened stakes set into the bottoms of the pits and trenches. The torches illuminated the scene in a hellish light.

"Pity about the horses," Wulf said.

"No help for it," Falcon answered.

"I suppose it's too much to hope that Valdemar is out there," Wulf sighed.

"I hope he is not. I want him for myself. Impalement on a stake is too good for him, even if he stays out there alive all night. But, he wouldn't risk himself in a night attack where he's as vulnerable as an ordinary soldier." He took a last look at the field, where wounded men were being helped onto horses and the line of horses was winding back toward the castle. "I'm going back to bed."

The next morning, siege work began in earnest. As soon as dawn arrived, the trebuchets thundered to life, casting great stones against the walls. Their trajectory was too high to hit the outer walls, so Rupert aimed at the keep. The idea was to strike the central tower and send the stone rebounding among the men below in the bailey. Sometimes the stone would fragment, sending shards whizzing among the men and causing many more wounds than any solid stone. Rupert continually lamented that he had no blocks of flint, plentiful in northern France but rare here; they were ideal for this purpose.

Gradually, chunks began to fall away from the keep. This was good for morale, and cheers greeted every fallen stone, but it was useless militarily. The tower was so massive that it would take months for such bombardment to have any serious effect.

Under Guido's direction, the archers tried potshots at the men on the walls. For this purpose, mantlets were used to get the men within bowshot. These were tall shields carried before each archer by an assistant. When planted on the ground with its supporting pole, the mantlet was large enough to protect both men from missiles. A few unwary men were picked off in this fashion, but it was easy to see the arrows and bolts coming, and the archery served more as a sport for the bowmen and a diversion for the watchers than as any serious nuisance.

At noon, after a good meal and plenty of preparation, Falcon ordered the first assault. With more than half the force, he attacked the main gate. At the same time, Rupert took an independent force to batter at the weak corner.

On foot, with shield and ax, Falcon stood beside the shed which held the battering ram, watching his men get into position. He climbed the ladder attached to the side of the shed and climbed onto its hide roof. He raised the ax, whirled it high overhead, and brought it down and forward, pointing to the castle. The trumpets blew, the drums began their beat, the men shouted and cheered. The shed began its slow, ponderous roll toward the gate.

By the time they were halfway there, arrows began landing around Falcon, and he raised his shield overhead. Several thunked into the leather-covered wood of the shield. Here and there, men were falling on the field.

"Keep your shields up!" he shouted, but amid the noise few heard him. Soon he was near enough for rocks to begin landing on the shed, and it was time to climb off. Hot oil would be next. Relentlessly, the shed crashed into the gate. Falcon went inside and started the ram swinging with the rhythm that would slowly batter its way through the massive, iron-strapped wooden gate and the stones stacked behind it by the defenders. "Heave! Heave!" Falcon took a rope himself and helped to haul back on the ram, then leaning forward to pull in the opposite direction to aid its impetus.

With every blow, the gate and the wall trembled. Great dents began to form on the timber of the door. The noise was incredible; the shouting and chanting of the men, the thunder of the ram, the steady racket of stones and other missiles striking the roof, all contributed to the din.

There came a stink of burning leather. Hot oil or pitch was being poured on the roof. Falcon looked up to make sure that none was leaking through. Shield high, he left the shed, using the opening at the back to avoid the hot oil.

Outside, the cacophony was as great. Men were screaming, stones cracked against shields, huge rocks continued to smash into the keep.

Falcon's men were having little luck in placing ladders against the wall. The defenders pushed them away with long forked poles. Vats of oil and pitch were ranged along the top of the wall, smoking ominously. Shield high and toward the wall, Falcon walked toward the southeast corner, where Rupert's sappers were under the cover of a series of sheds that hugged the base of the wall.

Falcon found Rupert directing a team of pick-and-hammer men who were working away at the sharp angle of the wall. Already it was crumbling under the assault. He caught sight of Falcon and waved his leader over.

"Welcome to the hall of the wall-smasher's guild, my

lord," Rupert called. He turned to the hammer men beside him. "Work those hammers, ye buggering turd-lickers, or Sir Draco'll shove 'em up yer bungholes and let you swing 'em that way!" The men grinned and swung all the harder.

Falcon inspected the progress. "How long?" he asked.

"Three days, at least," Rupert replied. Falcon cursed.

"I'd hoped for better. I'm going to go out and call the laddermen off. For now, we'll concentrate on the ram and the tunnel. I'll send some of them here and you can work them in reliefs. From now on, we work through the night."

"Very well, my lord," Rupert said.

Falcon left the shed and found his trumpeter. He had the signal for the ladder men's retreat sounded. The men carried their ladders back to the camp, and Falcon divided them into relief details to man the sapping sheds and the ram. He found his seneschal and ordered that there be no stinting the food and wine and ale while the assault was going on. Boys carried skins of watered wine to the men who were sweating so profusely in the sheds, and joints of flesh seethed in pots over the cookfires of the camp. When a team was relieved, it staggered wearily back to the camp to eat and drink and, if possible, to sleep.

Falcon sat wearily on his camp stool, cup in hand. How many sieges had he been involved in? The list reeled away in his mind, each castle and city with its unique horrors that burned in the memory. Was Acre the worst? It was certainly the biggest and longest. This siege of Pierre Noir was almost comically small by comparison. But then, events in the Holy Land were always on a greater scale than those in Europe.

The next day was much like the first. The ram thudded, the men shouted and cursed, the picks and hammers slowly ate into the wall. Rupert was carving a large tunnel, for the wall was thick and a sizable breach was necessary. When it was large enough, it was packed with wood and brush soaked in oil and the flammables were set alight. All through the next night the fire burned while Falcon ordered the men to get as much rest as they could. He called off the ram party, for it seemed as if the gate had been backed by solid masonry, and he wanted every man rested and ready for the assault on the morrow.

Falcon stood atop the tower. It had been moved up so close that an occasional arrow smacked into its draw-bridge. Nine other men crowded the small platform from which the storming party would cross the bridge to the wall. Rupert had assured him that it would be soon now. There were two other towers. Ruy was in charge of one of them, the Austrian knight Sir Rudolph the other. Falcon would have put Wulf and Donal in charge of them, but the knights insisted on the "honor" of being first atop the wall. Since it made not a bit of difference anyway, Falcon had agreed in the interests of morale.

He shoved his way to the edge of the tower and gazed at the ground, thirty feet below. Varlets were packing the axles with thick, foul-smelling grease. As the tower surged forward, these men would have to walk ahead of it, clearing stones from the path of the wheels. Many of them would be killed, but there was never a shortage of peasants.

A stiff wind blew up and the tower creaked. Only a few iron bolts had been used in its construction. The rest had been lashed together. Iron nails were too scarce to waste on a temporary structure like this, and when the siege was over it would be burned in order to recover the bolts.

The men sat on the ground, as they had all morning, their faces nervous and alert. Skins of heavily watered wine passed from hand to hand, and weapons were tested for sharpness for the thousandth time. Many of them would die this day, and they knew it well.

A crash of masonry drew every gaze to the southeast corner of the wall. A huge cloud of dust obscured vision, and every man leaped to his feet to see better. Gradually, the dust cleared and revealed a gaping breach in the corner. A vast cheer went up, and Rupert preened himself and graciously accepted the compliments that were shouted out to him.

"Forward!" bellowed Falcon, and the warcry went up as the oxen lurched forward against their traces. With a shuddering, swaying heave, the tower began inching its way to the wall. Falcon knew that the thing was sound—he had been in dozens of them—but its tottering progress and rickety feel frayed his nerves raw. Better to be on the ground and surrounded by enemies than committed to this frail man-made object.

A hundred paces from the wall, the tower's drawbridge was struck by a rock shot from a mangonel mounted on the wall. The little catapults were notoriously inaccurate, so it had to be a lucky hit. Falcon scanned the field to make sure that the other towers were keeping pace. For the maximum effect, it would be best if all three drawbridges dropped simultaneously. It was the ideal and it almost never happened, but it was always striven for. Working against it were factors of chance and terrain, but worst of all was the urge of knights everywhere to be the first on the wall and gain all the honor and glory. That factor, at least, Falcon could keep under control.

They were getting close now. No more than twenty paces. A grappling hook came sailing in and wedged one of its tines against the top edge of the drawbridge. A team of men hauling on its rope along the wallwalk could topple the tower.

"Shit!" Falcon gave his shield to a soldier and scrambled to the top of the drawbridge, which slanted slightly out from the vertical position. Grasping the top edge, he hauled himself over its lip. Immediately, arrows began to fall around him. One glanced from the shoulder of his mail. The rope stretched taut from the hook and men were straining at it. The tower began to tilt. With a sweep of his ax, Falcon severed the rope just as a fist-sized rock clanged from his helmet. The tower luched back upright and Falcon tumbled down the face of the bridge.

He got to his feet and took his shield again. The tower shuddered to a halt as its wheels stopped against the foot of the wall. The drawbridge was cut loose, but it did not fall. Men on the wall were holding it shut with poles. Falcon and his companions pushed against it with their shields. Slowly, it began to give way. Then it fell with a crash. Yelling and cheering, Falcon and his party stormed across and onto the wall.

The fighting was fierce, the quarters close. It was for this reason that Falcon chose the ax. A man cut at his leg and he dropped his shield a few inches to take the blow as he hewed downward at the man's exposed shoulder. The ax sheared through mail and flesh and the man fell screaming into the bailey.

Another took his place and lunged with a spear. Falcon blocked with his shield and caught the man's shield with the angle formed by blade and handle of the ax. He yanked the shield away from the man's body and stepped in, bringing the rim of his own shield up under the man's chin. As the man staggered back, Falcon's ax split his face.

Falcon surveyed the wall. He crouched and moved warily, for the wallwalk was littered with bodies and weapons and slick with blood. The greatest danger in a fight was to lose your footing, for a man on the ground rarely got up again. One of the other towers was disgorging its load of fighting men onto the wall about twenty paces from where Falcon was. On the other side, the third tower still could not lower its drawbridge. Falcon pointed to it. "They need help over there!" His men fought their way along the wall, taking the men resisting the third tower from behind. After a brief struggle, the bridge was down and more of Falcon's forces were on the wall. He could see a few of his men fighting in the bailey, which meant that the breach had been forced. The wall was quickly secured and Falcon's standard planted on its battlement. Even above the noise of battle could be heard the cheers from the camp, where the wounded and the noncombatants were watching with avid interest.

Leaving his ax on the wall, Falcon drew Nemesis and descended a stair to join the fight in the bailey. Here there was more room and better footing, and he was able to employ his favorite style of methodical, strength-saving cutting. The defenders were locking shields and backing toward the keep.

With so many shields so close together, it became difficult for Falcon to cut with his sword, and for an instant he regretted leaving his ax behind. He scanned the ground for a fallen ax or morningstar or other weapon useful for getting at men behind shields. Then he reminded himself that he was a leader and should be overseeing the operation, not losing himself in the mania of battle. He looked for Valdemar, and finally spotted him, standing by the gate of the keep and waving his men inside. Falcon leaped back into the fight with redoubled fury, wielding a morningstar he'd found and urging his men on. The more they killed before the enemy could shelter in the keep, the easier would be the next stage of the battle.

The portcullis came down, trapping outside the last defenders who had not been able to push their way in. These were cut down without mercy as stones and spears rained down from above, killing attacker and defender indiscriminately. Falcon signaled his men to fall back on the wall.

The wall was still within arrow range of the keep, but as soon as it was secured, Rupert had set about erecting roofs and screens to protect the men who would be working and camping there for the next stage of the siege.

"What are your orders for the night, my lord?" Rudolph of Austria asked.

"All men to rest except those on watch." Falcon sat on his folding camp stool, weary to the bone. He'd had his tent set up just outside the wall near the breach, which was even now being cleared of rubble to make an easy way in and out of the bailey. The masonry was also being cleared from the gate, the hinges of which were so battered that it might have to be burned or hewn apart. "The watchword will be . . ." He thought for a moment, then smiled. "It will be, 'Long live the Pope.'"

Even the dour Austrian had to smile at that. "The boys will enjoy that, sir. Attack again in the morning?"

"No, we'll rest for three days. Give them time to brood and get careless in there. That fool Thibaut will be driving Valdemar mad, and that's all to the good."

The Austrian left and Falcon poured himself a cup of wine, this time unmixed with water. He was sore all over and would need his sleep. Wulf awaited outside the door of the tent, and Falcon called him in. "Wulf, is everything prepared for our little sortie?"

"All ready, my lord. When do we go? Surely not tonight!"

"Sweet Jesus, no," Falcon laughed. "I couldn't climb into a wench's bed just now, much less a castle. We'll go three nights from now. Meantime, make sure that the men stay sober and that none sneak back to the whores in the camp."

"Our men will be no problem," Wulf said. "But the

137

levies from La Roche and the newcomers will never understand discipline."

"They don't count," Falcon said. "My own men are the only ones that concern me, because they're the only ones I depend on. The rest are rabble. For the most part, all they're good for is to intercept the odd stone or arrow that might otherwise hit one of my men."

"Some of them fought well, Draco," Wulf objected.

"Any man can fight well one day and turn tail like a coward the next. The only type to count on is the one who'll fight well every day, in good weather or bad, whether his side is winning or losing. We've both seen too many heroes in a victorious advance. How many do you see on a retreat?"

"Few," Wulf admitted.

"Remember those long marches in Palestine, when we'd abandoned one castle and were falling back to the next, with Saracen horsemen harrying us all day under the hot sun and the arrows falling all around? Damn few heroes then, but we had men who would retreat and hold their ranks and defend the next castle as they had the last. That's real soldiering, Wulf, not the kind of glorious foolery that Ruy and Rudolph and the others believe in." He took a drink of wine, savoring its sweetness.

"But that's Palestine," Wulf said. "It would never work here."

"Why not?" Falcon asked. "Only because every king and baron in Christendom outside Outremer depends on landholding knights and levies, and he can only call them up for forty days' service out of the year. With land to tend to, who can give more time? But an army whose trade is nothing but war is not tied to planting and plowing and harvesting. With my men under my control year round I can train and drill and discipline them until they're as good as the best in Outremer."

"I don't know," Wulf said doubtfully. "It's never been done before."

"It's being done now," Falcon said. He got up from the stool and dropped onto his bed. "I'm going to sleep now. See that I'm not disturbed."

Something woke him. His instincts told him that it was past the middle of the night. Had it been a sound? His eye caught movement in the tent, and he froze. Whoever they were, they knew from his breathing that he was awake and must strike quickly. He rolled from the bed just as a dagger came down where he had been lying.

He hit the floor rolling and snatched up Nemesis from where it had been lying next to him. A man stood over him, and he kicked his feet from under him, bringing the man to the ground. Rising to one knee, he could dimly see the other man against the tent wall, which glowed from the light of a campfire outside. He tore Nemesis from its sheath and sliced upward in one motion, cleaving the man from crotch to sternum. The man was all but naked and he opened like a ripe melon.

Pivoting on his knee, Nemesis held overhead, Falcon brought the sword down on the other intruder. He felt the blade connect and go deep, but the man was swinging something and it came down on Falcon's bare head. Before he lost consciousness, he only had time to hope that there had been no more than two intruders in his tent.

The young men had been wandering for days. Every time they came near to where they thought they might find King Guy and his army, they had seen parties of Saracen horsemen. They could not risk capture, so they spent most of their time in hiding. They were tired and hungry, but most of all they were fearful of what might be happening to the army.

They climbed a rise in the ground just at dusk and saw

139

thousands of campfires spread out below them. It had to be the Crusader army. They spurred it. Somewhere down there were King Guy and Raymond of Tripoli, the Templars and their grand master, Gerard of Ridefort.

At the edge of the camp, a sentry challenged them. "Halt and give the password!"

"How should I know it?" Falcon fumed. "I've been separated from the army for days."

"Then you'll have to wait till morning," the soldier said.

"But I have to see King Guy now!" Falcon cried. "I'm Squire Draco de Montfalcon, and I bear important news!"

"Never heard of you," the soldier said phlegmatically, and Draco prepared to draw his sword and cut the fool down.

He was stopped in this rash act by the arrival of the captain of the watch. "What's all this noise?" he asked. Draco identified himself. The captain raised his torch to see better.

"Young Draco, is it? Yes, there's only one white streak like that in the army. Come with me. I can't take you to the king, but I'm Raymond of Tripoli's man, and I can let you see him." Gratefully, Draco followed.

Raymond's tent was in the center of his quadrant of the camp, next to King Guy's and separated from the camp of the Templars, with good reason. Raymond and Gerard, grand master of the order, had been deadly enemies for many years.

Raymond of Tripoli, Prince of Galilee, looked up as the captain ushered Draco into the tent. Like most of the Crusading generals, he was a big, powerful man, trained from boyhood upward in the wearing of armor and the wielding of heavy weapons. Usually a jovial man, he now looked harried and harassed.

"Ah, young Draco," he said. "What is it? And where's Eudes? We've been searching for your father for days."

"Sir, I must speak to you alone." Struck by Draco's serious tone and ragged appearance, Raymond dismissed the guard captain.

"Now, what is it?"

In a breathless rush, Draco told his story, from the conference he had interrupted in the castle to his head-long flight. During the recitation, Raymond's face went alternately scarlet and pale. He had him repeat the part about the big Frank who tried to stop them and whom Wulf had wounded.

"You say he swore 'by God's whisker's'?"

"Yes, my lord. Why? Do you think you know him?"

"All too well. Many things that were obscure are now clear. There was a conference of the leaders of the Crusade two nights past. I counseled that we take up a defense at Saffuriyeh, where there's water and communication by sea with Acre, but you know how heavy my advice weighs with King Guy." There was no love lost between the two.

"Renaud of Chatillon was there. It was his attack on a Moslem party traveling under my safe-conduct that started this war, just when we had worked out a good treaty with Saladin. Gerard was there too. Even so, I had the king swayed. He agreed to stay at Saffuriyeh. The meeting broke up.

"Next morning, I awoke to find that he'd changed his orders during the night. That morning, we set out on this march. It was Gerard who talked Guy into it when I could not interfere." He looked at Draco sadly. "Gerard's favorite oath is 'by God's whiskers.' And for the last few days, he's worn his arm in a sling."

Draco's mind reeled. The grand master of the Templars, the most illustrious of the Crusading orders, a traitor? His faith in the Crusade and its leadership was crumbling fast.

"We have to warn the king!" Draco urged.

"No use," Raymond said. "He'd never take the word of an untried boy against that of the grand master of the Templars. You know, Draco, you're regarded with no little suspicion in this army, because of the way the lightning marked you."

Wearily, Raymond got to his feet. "It's in God's hands now. I can fight my enemies, but who can save me from the treachery of my allies and the fickleness of a king?" He clapped Draco on the shoulder. "Go to that chest over there. One of my squires died of the bloody flux a few weeks ago. His hauberk's in there. Take it. Tomorrow, stay near my banner. If we're both alive a week from now, I'll knight you myself."

"Thank you, my lord," Draco said, numb with despair.

"Well, at least we'll be able to ease your mind of one burden."

"What is that, my lord?"

"We should be able to recover your father's body for burial. The army marches into Hattin tomorrow."

NINE

WULF was bathing the side of his head with wine and vinegar when he came to. For a few moments, Falcon groped for orientation in the unfamiliar surroundings of the tent. Then the memories came flooding back. One wall of the tent was soaked in blood from side support to ground, and the dirt floor was awash with it, but there were no bodies present.

Wulf followed his gaze. "Nemesis is a messy tool," he observed.

"Good for fighting in the dark, though," Falcon said. "Who were they?"

"Valdemar's two Saracens. I had the bodies dragged outside. One of them fetched you a clout with a candlestick before he fell."

With a hand to his throbbing head, Falcon climbed shakily to his feet and went outside, blood making his progress sticky. The bodies were stretched out beneath the torch of a guard. The men outside were relieved to see their leader alive and apparently not too much the worse for his experience. The story was already spreading through the camp of how he had killed two attackers in the dark with two blows, one of them at the same instant that the man was striking him down. He crouched to examine the bodies, breathing through his mouth to avoid

143

the stench of spilled entrails. He could see nothing that might indicate that they had belonged to the fanatical sect of the Assassins.

"What shall we do with 'em, my lord?" asked Rupert, who had come at the alarm. "Bury 'em like Christians?" Gravedigging came under Rupert's realm of expertise, since he was in charge of all pick-and-shovel work.

"No. At first light, load them into the trebuchet and fire them into the keep. Think you can land them on the roof so they slide down onto the wallwalk?"

"Oh, aye!" Rupert said, slapping his thigh and nearly choking with mirth. "That'll be a fine jest, just the thing to set the men in a good humor. Them buggers inside'll fart blue flames to see thee standing on the wall in the morning and these two shit-skins come aslidin' down the roof! I'll sew 'em up so's they don't come all apart in the air."

Chuckling gleefully, the old man had the bodies dragged away. Falcon had his tent struck and set up on a new site, as he didn't want to wake up in the midst of all the flies that would be attracted to the blood-soaked ground. The bloody wall of the tent was washed down with vinegar and water and it was fit for habitation once more. Falcon resumed his interrupted sleep, fervently hoping for no more such disturbances.

Thibaut sipped morosely at his wine. Shut up in the keep three days and his nerves were already frayed. Two mornings before, he'd been standing atop the keep waiting to see the consternation in the enemy camp when Falcon was to have been discovered dead in his tent. True, Valdemar's Saracens had not yet returned, but the German had said that they might hide out in the forest until the next night.

First light had revealed Draco Falcon standing on the captured outer wall, hands on hips and smiling up at him.

There had been a shout from the watch, and he had stared, horrified and unable to move, as two large objects came spinning through the air from the big trebuchet. They had passed above his head, and he'd hunched his shoulders as he awaited the inevitable smash of the stones against the lead sheeting of the peaked roof.

Instead, there had been a tremendous splat, and what had rained down on him had not been rock fragments but a foul porridge of Saracen that had begun to stink in the warm summer weather. Valdemar had turned crimson and shouted curses at the smiling figure below, and Thibaut had ordered his archers to shoot at the man. Then the daily bombardment of stones had begun and he'd scurried back into the safety of the keep.

"I was right," Thibaut was saying. "He bears a magic sword. It protects him and strikes in the dark. My barber-surgeon examined the bodies of your two Saracens. There was enough of them left to tell that each was killed by a single blow. One was split from shoulder to waist, the other cut upward from privates to breast. You hear that? Struck from below! What more proof do you need that the sword was guided by an imp, doubtless reaching upward by magical means to guide the blade directly from hell?"

Valdemar sighed. Why did he bother? "My lord," he explained patiently, "if you had been attacked in as many black alleys from Byzantium to Alexandria as he and I have, you too would be adept at the art of fighting in the dark. As for the upward blow, it's called the ballsplitter, and it's common in the East. I've only seen it done with daggers and short swords, though, never with a big cleaver like the one he carries. Wish I'd seen how he did it." The German took a heavy swallow of wine. "There are no magic swords, my lord. If there were so much as one in all Christendom, I'd own it by now."

"You and your boasting! You were supposed to kill

him in the trial by combat, and you failed. All you did was get me excommunicated and give my neighbors an excuse to attack me. Your Saracens were supposed to kill him, and you failed me again. Tell me, sir knight, just what have you done to earn your pay?"

Gently, Valdemar smiled as he leaned across the table separating him from his liege. Thibaut shrank back in his seat as the German thrust his face to within an inch of Thibaut's. "What I have done, my sweet little lord, has been to help you raid your neighbors, at your orders, with such reckless greed that they have banded together for the kill, as I predicted.

"If you'd followed my advice, we'd have abducted Marie de Cleves months ago and you could have forced marriage on her, thus gaining her whole estate. That way, you could have been happily sweating atop your pretty cousin this very minute, instead of waiting out a siege that could go on for months. All your troubles are the result of your own greed, cowardice and vacillation. You have never seen fit to take my advice. If you had, you'd be the greatest lord in the district right now instead of the cowering, excommunicate holder of one miserable keep!" Valdemar poured himself more wine and calmed himself with a visible effort.

"If, however," the German went on, "you are so dissatisfied with my performance as to wish to dispense with my services, you need merely release me from my oath and I will be down the wall on a rope and away as soon as it's dark. My liege," he added.

"No, no, captain," said Thibaut, all asweat. "Please, do not be offended at my words. Sometimes, under the stress of pressing events, I speak overhastily. I am of course completely satisfied with your services, which have been those of a great captain and valiant knight. I repose full faith in your ability to clear up this little matter of the siege, then doubtless a little diplomacy with Rome, along with some gifts in that direction, and this misunderstanding which led to my excommunication will be taken care of, and you and I can go on as before."

Valdemar smiled once more. "Now," he said, "my lord speaks like himself again!"

Falcon and his party assembled at the foot of the keep wall. Rupert had assured him that his was a blind spot, visible from no part of the battlement. To make sure, Falcon had his men celebrating around a huge bonfire set out on the field just out of missile range. This would occupy the sentries' attention and keep them partially night-blinded with its glare. The sound of lutes and singing came eerily from beyond the outer wall of the besieged fortress.

The little party moved about its business quietly and without wasted effort or fumbling. They had been rehearsing this operation for days and each knew what he was to do.

Falcon, who had the longest and strongest throwing arm, cast the grapple up to the battlement sixty feet above. All but the tips of the hook had been swathed in cloth. Still, the clunk it made in landing was quite audible below. Had it been heard above, or were the sentries too distracted by the din in the field to notice? Falcon tugged on the rope. The hook was firmly seated. There was no further noise from above.

Guido, smallest of the group and the most agile climber, ascended the rope like a monkey. They waited tensely below. If the guards had found the grapple, they'd wait until the climber reached the battlement and then cut his rope and chuckle while the wretch fell. Falcon was prepared to ram Guido with his shoulder should he fall. Sometimes that would slow a man's fall enough so that he got off with a few broken bones. If the move was badly timed, both men would be killed.

Guido made it over the battlement. They let out a collective sigh. Falcon waited, hand on the rope, while Guido took stock of the situation above, ready to dagger a sentry or two should it be necessary. He felt two tugs, a wait, then two more.

Falcon went up next, Nemesis slung over his back. Like the rest, he was unarmored, a disadvantage demanded by the stealth necessary to his mission. Arrived on the battlement, he stood beside Guido, flexing his arms and waiting for the others to arrive. A guard lay at their feet in a widening pool of blood.

The others arrived; Wulf, Donal, Simon, the chain of his morningstar muffled, and the ax thrower, a man named Gerd. Silently, they made their way along the battlement in search of a door leading downward into the keep. Falcon held up his hand, and they stopped. A sentry bearing a spear and a wooden buckler was leaning on the parapet, staring intently at the fire on the field. Falcon signaled Simon to go forward and deal with the man.

Nonchalantly, as if he had every reason for being there, Simon walked over to the man. The sentry wheeled at the sound of footsteps. He squinted with night-blinded eyes to see who it was. "Who are you? Is it Pierre? Get back to your post, you fool! The captain—" With a flick of the wrist, Simon snapped the iron ball forward. The long spike sank into the wood of the shield with a slight thunk. Simon jerked the shield away from the man's body. The sentry opened his mouth, about to call out, but the edge of Simon's buckler smashed into his throat and a boot in his stomach doubled him over. As the man bent forward, Simon brought the iron shield rim down on the back of his neck. As the party passed, Simon heard Donal whisper: "Not bad for a monk."

The door was a low one, let into the wall and well protected by the lead-sheathed roof. Falcon was about to try it when he heard the faint sound of footsteps from the other side. He waved his men back and they flattened themselves against the wall, seeking invisibility in the shadowed overhang of the roof. The door opened and an armored man came through, followed by four others. It was the change of the guard mount. As they passed the raiding party, hands grabbed their arms and covered their mouths and daggers flashed in the light of the bonfire. When the bodies were lowered to the stone, Falcon knelt and felt their faces. There was no mustache as large as Valdemar's. Falcon signaled Guido and Donal to come near. In a low whisper he told them: "There must be two more sentries. Go kill them before they wonder what happened to the relief."

About ten minutes later the two returned, wiping their knives, and the party started gingerly down the stair, Falcon in the lead. Like all castles, Pierre Noir was designed to be defended room by room, floor by floor, but it was designed against attack from below, not above. All the doors bolted from the back, to be shut against an enemy who had forced a way through the main doorway on the ground floor. For this reason, the stairways of the castle spiraled to the right as one ascended, thus cramping the sword arm of the climbing attacker, while allowing the defender above the outer arc of the stairwall for the traverse of his weapon. By attacking from above, Falcon reversed this order. If they were met on the stair, the advantage lay with them. All doors could be opened easily.

The stair debouched into a small guardroom. Two off-duty guards sat at a table drinking. They looked up and goggled as Falcon came striding into the room, then Nemesis flashed across both throats in a single swipe. The next room was crowded with men, as rooms in besieged castles tended to be. They stirred sleepily as Falcon strode across the room and planted himself at the door, Nemesis held in both hands. Some stirred to life and called out, and there was a general struggle for weapons as the raiding party came into the room like invading demons. Morningstar, ax, falchion, sword, and dagger flashed among them as they cried and shouted, many of them killing one another in their confusion. Some tried to escape, but Falcon cut down all who tried to flee his way and Donal held the other door with his ax. In the space of a minute or two, twenty men lay dead in the straw. None of the attackers bore worse than nicks. The thick walls and doors of the castle ensured that no sound had been heard outside the room.

The room opened onto a corridor, and they walked the long hallway without trying to tiptoe, for now their trust was best put in boldness rather than stealth. Several crowded rooms opened off the corridor, but no one inside so much as looked up, for a castle under siege was full of comings and goings.

From the corridor a stairway angled down the wall of the great hall. This was tricky, because the stair was completely open and the hall lit with torches. They sauntered down the stair, yawning, weapons held carelessly, like men summoned from sleep to perform some errand. Falcon held his sword beneath his arm toward the wall so that its distinctive shape would not be noticed. A couple of sleepy pages looked up, then lowered their heads once more. The men asleep on the straw on the floor snored on without a care in the world. Even the dogs remained sleeping. Sleep could be cultivated as a fine art in a castle under siege. Men got so that they could sleep twenty hours a day, since there was precious little else to do.

They crossed the hall and found another stair leading downward. With the spiral stairs, it was difficult to keep their orientation. Falcon knew which side of the keep he wanted to end up at, but damned if he knew which way he was facing when he left the stair.

The rooms and corridors were much smaller in the

150

lower stories. For strength, the walls had to be thickest at this level, and to support the weight of the edifice, the inner walls had to be likewise stout. In these narrow passages, Nemesis was too long a weapon to be useful, so Wulf took the lead with his falchion and Falcon drew his dagger.

Finally, they found what they were looking for. It was a room larger than most this low down. The reason for its greater size was the presence of the machinery it had to house. In the center of the room was a huge, drumlike affair wrapped with chains and having a large windlass at each end. It was the mechanism for raising the heavy portcullis that blocked the main gate of the keep. Two men slept by the machine, and they never woke up.

Falcon and his companions picked up the turning spokes from their racks and thrust their squared ends into the holes of the windlasses. Three men took each end and they began to haul slowly back. The ratchet hook began to creep slowly up the curved outer surface of the cog on the stop wheel. It crept over the top, then snapped down into the reverse notch with an emphatic clack.

Gunther Valdemar awoke on the straw-stuffed sack that served him for a bed. He shoved the snoring kitchen girl away from him and sat up, alert for the sound to come again. There it was! A slow clack-clack-clack. It seemed to be coming from outside. He got up and crossed over to the arrow slit, men on the floor cursing as he stumbled over them. He leaned into the slit and cocked an ear outward. It was clearer now, and it seemed to be coming from below the slit somewhere. Then he went cold all over as he realized what it was.

"To arms!" he bellowed. "Off your arses and arm! The bastards are in the keep and they're raising the portcullis!" He stormed about the room, kicking men awake, shoving weapons in their hands, and sending them out to raise the garrison. He struggled into his own hauberk and clapped on his helmet. With an ax in his fist, he went with a party of men to take the gate room. He sent nobody to rouse Thibaut.

When the clamor came faintly to their ears, they redoubled their efforts, no longer trying to suppress the noise of the ratchet. It was back-breaking effort, ordinarily calling for the labor of at least ten men, but they were desperate. When the portucllis was almost up, they heard axes chopping at the door. Their pulling at the spokes was frantic now. Then the top of the portcullis began to come up through the long slit in the floor. Wulf drove its retaining wedge into place while Falcon leaned out an arrow slit and blew a long blast on his hunting horn. Then the door gave way and the defenders were coming in.

The men waiting under the roofs atop the outer wall fingered their weapons and wondered what had become of Falcon and the others. They had been gone a long time. Every man except for the small but noisy bonfire detail was waiting under the roofs or just outside the breached corner. They awaited the signal, if it was going to come.

Ruy Ortiz stood in the shadow of the wall so he would not be noticed by the sentries above, if any were still alive. He should have been under the roofs too, but he didn't want to yield any advantage to Rudolph of Austria, who, when the signal came, could simply dash through the breach and across the bailey and reach the gate first. It was only fair that Ruy should descend the wall ahead of his men and have a chance at the honor of being first into the gate. Of course, even more honor would go to those who had made the daring climb into the castle, but Falcon had been right not to let Ruy and Rudolph go along as they had begged to. Only knights of rank should lead the ground attack. Then he heard the horn.

"St. James and Lord Draco!" Ruy bellowed, and he ran toward the gate, sword in both hands. He glanced to one side. Rudolph was almost even with him! The cheat had been waiting *inside* the breach, in defiance of orders! Then it was a footrace between Ruy and Rudolph to get to the gate first, well ahead of their men. Defenders were beginning to crowd the portal.

The two knights reached the gate simultaneously, and they plowed among the defenders like an unstoppable mowing machine. The two huge blades, Ruy's Moorslayer and Rudolph's Cheeseparer, whirled in flashing circles, leaving a litter of lopped limbs and spilled entrails. They actually had cleared the gate by the time their men caught up with them.

With a crash of splintered fragments, the door disintegrated and the first man-at-arms broke into the room. Gerd snatched a francisca, the ancient Frankish throwing ax, from his belt and sent it spinning across the intervening distance. The man-at-arms lurched back, the francisca buried in his forehead. He tripped the next two who tried to spill into the room, and Donal axed both as they fell. The bodies made an effective barrier. Anyone seeking to enter the room now had to scramble over them or vault them, in either case laying himself open to a killing blow from the men inside. The men outside the door were being urged on by the unmistakable voice of Gunther Valdemar.

"In there, you sons of whores! Don't let them get that grate up or we're all dead! Get through! Get through!"

Falcon pushed his way to the fore of his men and shouted: "It's up, Valdemar! If you want to drop it again, come in yourself! I'm waiting for you here!" He grasped Nemesis in both hands and swung a horizontal cut, taking out two more men who were pushing forward. The doorway was now blocked up to knee level and thus effectively sealed against men on foot, who could not enter except at a severe disadvantage. The main danger now was the arrival of bowmen. There were not enough blind corners for them all to hide in, and in any case missile troops could keep them pinned down long enough for the bodies to be dragged outside and the room stormed. Fortunately, the archers seemed to be elsewhere.

"Forget them for now!" Valdemar shouted. "Everyone down to the gate! Draco, I'll be back for you as soon as I've disposed of your rabble below!" Nothing loath, the men cleared from the door.

"We can get out, now, my lord," Gerd said.

"Not likely," Falcon answered. "Gunther Valdemar is not the man to leave an enemy like me behind his back. He'll have men posted outside the door."

Donal picked up one of the corpses from the floor by the belt and collar. He thrust it head first, through the door, jerking back the hand holding the collar. Instantly, a broad falchion descended, shearing off the head. "Right you are, my lord," the Irishman said.

"Onward, onward!" shouted Ruy Ortiz, cleaving a spearman with Moorslayer. They were forcing their way up the stair, the gate well behind them now. The caballero Ruy Ortiz had the untiring arms of a knight trained from birth to the greatsword, and his heavy mail took the force of most of the blows aimed at him, leaving him free to concentrate on his duty, the slaying of his liege's enemies. "We must find the gateroom and rescue Lord Draco. If I fall, go there and rescue him!" Nobody heard him, of course; they had concerns of their own. But if he fell in this assault, he wanted it to be remembered that Ruy Ortiz died doing the duty of a good vassal, trying to save his liege from the enemy. Visions of Roland at Roncesvalles and the Cid at Valencia ran through his head as he chopped men like sides of mutton.

On another stairway, Rudolph of Austria was having a fine time in clearing away the poorly armed rabble opposing him. Methodically, with little fuss, he carved them down, not wishing to tire himself overmuch, because he knew that there was some stiff fighting ahead when he would encounter some knights as well protected as he. "Down with that spear, now, you common swine," Rudolph said as he hacked the shoulder from the man. Then he had a clear way for a few steps and there, on a landing, was Gunther Valdemar.

"Sir Gunther," Rudolph called, delighted, "will you yield to me or do battle!"

"Oh, well, if I must," Valdemar said. Cheeseparer swung and Valdemar caught the hilt in the angle of his axhead, yanking Rudolph forward. He slammed his steel-scaled fist into the side of Rudolph's coif, just below the helmet rim. The Austrian knight went down like a dead ox, and Valdemar readied to hew his head away, but a one-eyed old fellow thrust a torch almost into his eyes and he was forced back.

"Not Sir Rudolph, ye infant-dorking shit-sniffer!" the old man said. "He looks too fine on parades for dragon puke like you to do him in."

The old fellow was uncommonly handy with a torch, and Valdemar began retreating up the stair. He came to a landing with a door and slammed it shut, throwing the bolts. He ran to find more men.

The men in the gateroom were beside themselves listening to the sounds of carnage filtering up the corridors but unable to take part themselves or even to know how the fight was faring. Then there was the din of a fight in the corridor outside. Men appeared before the door, locked in combat, then all was quiet for a moment.

Ruy Ortiz thrust his face over the pile of bodies heaped in the doorway, "My lord! You are safe and I have been

155

able to preserve you! I shall burn a hundred candles to the Virgin and St. James in gratitude!"

Another face appeared over the carnage, a grizzle-bearded, one-eyed face. "Look at them! Sitting here quiet as you please, with a thumb up their arse and t'other tickling their cods, while us poor men's a-hewing the shit from these buggers here. Come on out, my lord, we've made it safe for ye."

Falcon picked his way over the corpses, some of them still emitting death rattles and watery farts. "Where's Valdemar?" he asked.

"I have not seen him, my lord," said Ortiz.

"The page-pronger was on the stair down there, my lord," said Rupert, jerking a grimy thumb over his shoulder. "He bashed poor old Sir Rudolph in the head something terrible, but it takes more than such a pat to dent such a head, it being harder'n a Pope's—" Falcon shoved him out of the way and dashed for the stair. "But, my lord," Rupert called after him, "we've got your hauberk somewhere around here, don't go a-running off bare-butted!" The old man shrugged and went off with the others in pursuit of their leader.

Thibaut awoke to the clamor of battle. Heart in his throat, he rose and crossed to his chamber door. He opened it a crack and looked out over his wooden gallery outside and down into the floor of the great hall below. Men were fighting there. The enemy had penetrated his castle! He slammed the door. Cowering against the wall was the serving girl he'd taken to his bed this night. She was about fourteen and very small, but she might do.

"Come, girl, give me your dress," he ordered. The girl, numb with terror, seemed not to hear. Thibaut slapped her vigorously, and when she seemed not to notice he knocked her to the ground and kicked her head several times. When she lay quiet he stripped the poor dress from her thin body. Working frantically, he tore off his own garments and dressed in the shabby gown. He went to the door and peeked out again. There were no men on the gallery yet. He slipped out the door and made his way to the nearest stair, face to the wall.

Falcon broke into the hall, hewing away the two men who tried to hold the door. The greater part of the defenders were gathered here, bewildered and frightened, but armed and ready to resist.

"Valdemar!" Falcon shouted, ignoring the others, "Where are you? I've come to drink your blood!" An axman rushed at him and Falcon split him from right shoulder to left hip, and then his men were crowding into the hall and bellowing their bloodlust.

The crowding was too great for any kind of scientific fighting, and Falcon hewed with Nemesis in short chops. Soon men in the opposing mob were dropping their weapons and shouting "Quarter! Quarter!"

"Stop the killing!" Falcon shouted. "Cease slaying!" It took him several minutes of laying about him with Nemesis's flat to enforce his will, but Ruy quickly caught on and assisted him, while Wulf went about gathering up arms from those who had surrendered.

Valdemar was nowhere to be seen, and Falcon dashed off down a corridor to find him.

The prisoners were being herded from the hall, none too gently, when Rupert caught sight of a movement along one wall. A figure dressed in a girl's shift was inching toward a side door. Rupert dashed over and grasped a skinny shoulder. "There, my pretty! Trying to go somewhere?" He spun the figure around and burst into laughter. "My lord," he said, "if you'd be taken for a maid, best shave off thy beard first!"

"Good man," Thibaut said, bowels quaking, "I yield me to you. Take me to your lord and I'm sure he'll reward you richly." He tried to smile in an ingratiating manner.

"Why, for sure he will," said Rupert. "And thou'lt be rewarded as well. As you have so richly merited."

"Eh?" Thibaut said. With a hard yank, Rupert dragged Thibaut to a corner. in which was piled a heap of dog turd. Rupert flung him face down in the redolent pile.

Thibaut pushed himself up, much bemired, and lamented: "It was that German traitor who brought me to this! My misfortune began when I hired him."

Rupert put his foot on the back of Thibaut's neck and forced his face back down into the pile. "Nay, my lord," he said. "Thy troubles started when the dog fucked thy mother and made thee!" It was a long time before Thibaut stopped twitching.

Falcon went through every room he could find. Valdemar was nowhere to be found. Wulf caught up with him. Together, they started at the top of the castle and worked their way down. Then they instituted a systematic search, prodding every pile of straw with spears, breaking open every chest, looking down all the wells and privies.

Valdemar had vanished as if he had never been.

Gunther Valdemar rode as if the Devil were behind him. The comparison was apt. He cursed Falcon and he cursed Thibaut for being such a fool and he cursed himself for ever taking service with Thibaut.

He drew rein. What was the use? Even if he escaped, as he easily could, there would still be Draco Falcon at his back with an army. Best settle with him once and for all. It would be easiest, naturally, if Falcon was separated from his army, but how could that be done?

Above all, he wanted to hurt Falcon. After his father and the Turkish galley, though, what could still torment him? Then Valdemar smiled as the answer came to him.

TEN

FALCON turned the corpse over with his foot. The excrement-smeared features of Thibaut were clearly recognisable.

"Died as he lived, my lord," Rupert said. "Eating shit."

"Did he try to surrender?" Falcon asked.

"Can't say as to that, my lord," Rupert answered. "I'm getting fearful hard of hearing these days."

Falcon pressed it no further. He believed in giving quarter to fighting men who knew that further resistance was futile, but a human tick like Thibaut had no claim on such treatment. But where was Valdemar?

Wulf arrived. "Valdemar's escaped, my lord. He must have pretended to be one of our wounded and just walked out the gate as we were mopping up in the hall. He got back to the camp and stole a horse and rode away."

"God curse me for a fool!" Falcon cried. "Why didn't I post guards at the gate who knew the bastard by sight?" He cursed wildly, and for a moment Wulf was afraid that he would forget all of Suleiman's teachings and go into one of his old killing rages, when no man within sword's reach was safe.

But the rage drained out of Falcon and he sagged wearily. "Well, it's done. We'll take up pursuit as soon as it's light. Not much chance of finding him, though. He's wily as any fox. No matter. I'll catch up to him again. Him and the others. Gather all the plunder in the bailey and we'll divide it, then set torch to this place."

"My lord," Wulf said, "I don't think we've time for that. I think we should ride for La Roche now."

"La Roche? Why?"

"We left the place undefended, Draco. And Valdemar will want to do you a hurt before he leaves for good."

The color drained from beneath Falcon's weathered skin. "Marie!" he half whispered, then, shouting; "Marie!" He dashed from the castle in search of his horse, with Wulf close behind.

Valdemar rode up to the main gate of La Roche and scanned the walls. He had dreamed of taking this place by force or by guile and coercing Thibaut into giving it to him as reward for his services. With this small holding, he could have begun the rebuilding of his fortunes. Well, it was not to be. No matter, there were other places as good or better.

The lone sentry, a man with a limp, came up to him with a spear and demanded his business. As Valdemar had expected, he was not recognized. "I'm one of the volunteer soldiers who joined at the siege of Pierre Noir. I bring news to Lady Marie de Cleves." The man let him pass, and Valdemar rode to the keep.

Inside, a flock of ladies demanded news, but he said that the Lady Marie had to be informed first. He kept his head bowed, and in the dim light in the keep his face was hidden from anyone who might know him. One of the ladies offered to guide him to Marie's chamber, and he followed her up a narrow stair.

"Sir," the lady asked, "surely you can at least tell me whether Sir Rudolph of Austria still lives?" The woman was wringing her hands with anxiety.

"When last I saw him, he lived," Valdemar said.

"Oh, thank Jesus!" the lady said, crossing herself. She glanced at the knight beside her just as they passed one of the infrequent torches that illuminated the narrow hall. "My lady's door is that one there. Shall I . . ." Her voice trailed off as the torchlight caught the long mustaches, the battered face. "I know you." She said it almost as a question. "I saw you at the trial by combat." Her eyes went wide and she drew in breath to call out.

Valdemar clamped a hand over her mouth and shoved her against the stone wall. He held her there easily as he drew his dagger and placed it carefully beneath her left breast. He shoved it in, angling upward to pierce the heart and working the handle sideways two or three times to make sure. She died almost instantly and with no sound. He held her thus for a minute. To draw out the dagger too soon would send blood fountaining to the opposite wall of the hall, and he wanted to leave no evidence outside. His business in Marie's chamber might take some time.

Marie had been in her chamber without sleep all night, alternately praying and pacing. Falcon had hinted that something would be tried that might end the matter of Thibaut immediately. If she knew Draco, he would be in the thick of it instead of delegating the duty to an inferior like any other sensible captain.

She almost fainted when word came by troubador of the two Saracens in Draco's tent. The troubador who had brought the news had hoped to earn an extra reward by being first to arrive with a song about the event. While her ladies had bubbled over Draco's heroic strength and skill, Marie had fumed at Draco's rashness in pitching his tent beneath the very walls of an enemy castle and not posting enough guards to protect himself.

The knock at her door broke her reverie. She looked at her candle. It was yet early in the day. Perhaps it was news from Pierre Noir. She drew back the bolts of her door and tugged it open.

"Yes, what—" The door slammed open, throwing her back against the her bed. Something came hurtling through the doorway to land at her feet. Not quite understanding what was happening, she saw that it was one of her ladies. "Sara," she said, stupidly. "What have you done to Sara?" She looked up at the burly, armored figure who was slamming home the door bolts.

"I've killed her, of course, you silly bitch." He turned around, and her heart sank. Gunther Valdemar. She barely felt the backhanded blow that flung her back across her bed. She knew what was sure to happen next, but she could not feel much apprehension, or anything else except for a numb inner pain. If Valdemar was in the castle, then Draco Falcon must be dead.

Draco Falcon spurred his horse mercilessly. This was not his warhorse but a courser, a hunting beast trained to follow a running stag all day if need be. He knew that Valdemar would have instinctively taken a destrier, matchless for charging and fighting, but not as good for long-distance chasing.

One question was crucial: Had Valdemar ridden straight for La Roche when he left Pierre Noir, or had he ridden away in panic first and only later turned his steps toward La Roche? If the former, he was already too late and Marie was dead or worse. If the latter, there was still a bare chance. As he rode, he remembered. . . .

The Crusader army lay shattered in bloody ruin. It had been in the fields outside Hattin, beneath the twin crags called the Horns, that the Saracen army had lain in ambush. The scouts who rode ahead had given no warning. But then, Odo FitzRoy had been in charge of the scouts that morning.

Draco sat his horse near Raymond's banner, as he had been ordered, and Wulf was beside him. The clouds of choking dust obscured most of the battle, and it was as great a penance as the merciless sun. Dust, heat, and exertion generated a raging thirst in everyone, but they were cut off from water.

The fighting had been terrible, with the leaders mounting one charge after another, but the Saracens knew that they could not stand up to mailed Frankish cavalry, so they just faded away and shot their maddening storms of arrows.

Raymond of Tripoli rode up to his banner, his armor rent and blood leaking through. "We're breaking out of this!" he shouted. "The day is lost. If we don't go now, the horses will not be up to it later."

"But, my lord," one of the knights protested, "it isn't over yet! The Templars are hard pressed over there!" The man pointed to a rise of ground where the men in armor and white surcoats with red crosses were gathered around the Beauséant, the banner of the Temple. Saracens pressed them hard on all sides.

"The Templars are finished," Raymond said. "They've been betrayed by their own grand master." Men who heard this startling statement attributed it to Raymond's hatred of Gerard and did not take it seriously.

Hastily, the Crusaders formed into the "boar-head" array; a close-packed wedge of armored men and horses that could carve through an opposing force like a spearpoint.

The Saracens saw the iron triangle coming, and thought it another abortive charge by the knights. They fled before it as always, shooting back over their horses's rumps at the Crusaders, bringing down horses and men. This charge, though, did not stop. This time, the knights were not trying to come to grips with the Saracens. They were going to ride until they reached a place of safety.

Falcon rode on the right flank of the wedge, with Wulf riding on his left. They had fought all day and were exhausted and thirsty, but this was the last, supreme effort. Falcon would almost as soon have charged into the thick of the Saracen army and died, but his need for revenge drove him on. He had to live. He would not be able to rest until certain men died. His last sight of the battle was a side action occurring on a small knoll that the wedge passed just as they were getting clear of the Saracens. Draco saw a line of captured Templars, unhelmed and kneeling with their hands bound before them. The knight Gunther Valdemar was walking calmly down the line, stopping every pace or two to behead each man with his sword.

Then they were clear and riding for the coast. Raymond of Tripoli led the pitiful remnant of the great Crusading army that had set out from Saffuriyeh days before, to spread the word of the greatest disaster to occur in a century of the Crusades.

His horse was nearly dead when Falcon reached La Roche. He stormed past the guard, nearly trampling him and stopping only when the steed collapsed to its knees before the keep. He leaped clear of the saddle and ran up the steps and grabbed the first lady who came to the door to see what all the commotion was about.

"My Lord Falcon," she said, "what—" He grabbed her by the arms and lifted her clear of the floor in his fury.

"Where is Marie?"

"In her chamber, my lord," said the startled woman.

"Did a knight come here and ask to see her?"

"Yes, just a few minutes ago. My lord, what—" But he had already dropped her and was sprinting for the stair.

Before Marie's door he stopped. If he pounded on it and yelled, she would surely die, if she was alive now. The door was four inches thick and bolted with iron on the inside. It could take many minutes to hack through with an ax. He thought about the arrow slit. Could he reach that from the outside and shoot Valdemar with an arrow before he could finish whatever he was doing in there with Marie? Not a chance.

He leaned back against the wall opposite the door, closed his eyes, and, for the first time in years, tried to clear his mind and concentrate on the words said to him long ago by his teacher and second father, Suleiman the Wise.

We have seen how fanatical men such as the sect of the Assassins seem to be able to perform superhuman feats by the exercise of their faith or magic. But I say to you that there is no superhuman prowess and no magic. Allah does not allow such things. But to a man who believes in his faith and his cause, all things are possible. The strength is within, not without. Your Prophet's parable of the mountain and the mustard seed was a true one, for if a man believe in himself and his cause, no barrier can hold him and no weapon can stay him.

That had been early in his studies with Suleiman, and later the old man had taught him how to release the inner strength he had spoken of. It had not been easy to learn, and it was not to be done lightly. He took a deep breath and held it. He concentrated on the formula, *No barrier can hold him!* With a weird, high-pitched cry, he charged the door.

Valdemar regretted that he could not remove his armor, for Falcon might show up at any moment. This one was a pretty plum indeed. He had bound her to the bed and ripped her clothes off, none too gently. The side of her face was swelling where he had cuffed her upon entering, and her eye on that side was blackening and blood tricked from the corner of her mouth.

Well, if he couldn't rape her first, there were other things he enjoyed as much or more. He drew his dagger from Sara's body and wondered where to start. She seemed to be unconscious, though. It would not be as gratifying that way. He found a pitcher of water and dashed it over her. She shook her head a little, and he grasped her chin and forced her gaze upon him. He held the bloody dagger before her eyes.

"Can you guess what I'm going to do to you with this?" he asked in a gentle, crooning voice. Her eyes widened in pure horror, to his great satisfaction. He let his eyes roam her white body. "Let's see, where shall we start? Do you have any preferences, my lady?" She tried to speak, but all that came out was a strangled cry. "Here?" he said, prodding with the dagger point. "Or here?" Her muscles tensed to the point of cramping where the bloody iron touched her. "How about here?" he said, grasping and pulling cruelly. "Shall I cut one of these off? It would be a shame to ruin such a finely matched pair, but then shame is the least of what I shall do to you." He laid the edge of the dagger to her skin and pulled the soft flesh taut, preparing to cut. Then something unbelievable happened.

Something struck the door, and Valdemar's eyes were drawn to it in utter disbelief as he saw it bulge inward, then give way all in an instant and fly into hundreds of splinters as the twisted iron hinges and bolts slammed back against the wall and there stood Draco Falcon, and his big, curved sword was in his hands.

"No man can do that," Valdemar said matter-of-factly. For the first time since his youth, the German felt the cold talons of superstitious dread clawing at his bowels. "You've no ram, no ax," he went on. "What demon aids you?" He stood stupidly in the position he had been in when Falcon had struck the door, with his dagger in one hand and white flesh bulging from between the fingers of the other.

Nemesis flashed and somehow Valdemar was not surprised to see that his dagger blade had been clipped away at the hilt and the woman's flesh left untouched. Thrice more the blade flickered, so swiftly that the eye could not follow its movements, and Marie was free of her bonds. Valdemar waited for the next.

"Your sword, German pig." Falcon said. "Get it and fight me. I've waited too many years for this and I'll not kill you quickly like the swine you are."

Slowly, Valdemar drew the long, heavy blade. He took its handle in both hands and held it with its point menacing Falcon's throat. "Before we start," he said, "there is something that you should know, Draco de Montfalcon."

"And what is that?" Falcon said, blade held before his body.

"No," Valdemar said. "On second thought, I won't tell you. You'll have to make me tell you." Then he hewed at the side of Falcon's face, but Nemesis swept the blow aside. Falcon replied with an identical blow and laid the German's jaw open from ear to chin.

Valdemar began sweating heavily. "See, you treacherous bastard?" Falcon taunted. "This is what would have happened if you hadn't made Thibaut get this blade disqualified in the trial."

"You'll need more than a bewitched blade to kill me." Valdemar bragged, but his hand was not as steady as it had been, and his customary overweening self-confidence was seeping away. He chopped at Falcon's side, but the curved blade was there in the way and Falcon's riposte struck him in the ribs in the same spot he had been aiming at. The German knight grunted as the broad tip of Nemesis sheared through mail links and the padding beneath and into the flesh to the bone. He grunted and knew that his mail was now stained with blood.

"That could have been mortal," Falcon said. "All the way to your cowardly backbone. But you won't die as easy as that."

"For God's sake," Marie cried, still doubled up on the bed with the pain of her hurts, "finish him, Draco. This is not a game!"

But Falcon was not to be hurried. "I'm sorry, Marie," he said. "But this has been too long in coming." He was remembering too many things—his father's ruined body on the table in Valdemar's castle, the betrayal of Hattin, the years in the Turkish galley, many other things.

Valdemar was sweating now. The man was too good, the blade too sharp, and that door. . . . He searched his bag of tricks for a stratagem, something to throw this remorseless vengeance machine off its timing for just a bare moment, enough to be out the door and away.

"I remember your father, boy," he taunted. "Poor old Eudes. He was my good friend, you know." He saw Falcon's knuckles go white on Nemesis's grip, and he struck at that instant, a low blow to the knee, and it was blocked, but only just in time. Falcon's growing fury was costing him in calculation.

Falcon stood back and took a deep, calming breath. Then he was in and the curved blade was a blur and Valdemar was down on one knee. The knee tendon had been severed, and he could feel the warmth soaking his hose. Then he saw the Saxon at the door, and he knew that there was no escape. The choice now was between a slow death and a quick one. He placed his sword's point against the straw on the floor and leaned on the hilt.

"Poor old Eudes," he mused. "He gave us good sport while he lasted. He was a strong man, Eudes." Falcon growled and cut the other knee, sending the German back to sprawl in the straw. "I'd've done worse to this little bitch, though, if you hadn't interrupted." He didn't feel the next blow, but he knew it was a bad one. His plan was working.

On the bed, Marie was writhing and sobbing hysterically. Wulf rushed to her and wrapped her in a blanket and held her until she calmed a little.

"I had some fine plans for that one, all right," Valdemar said. "Already had a good time before you arrived, in fact. Do you remember our old friend Abu, and his idea of sport with young boys? Well, I served her the same way a little while back."

"It's not true!" Marie shrieked, but Falcon was beyond hearing. With a cry of pain and despair he clove Valdemar across the waist. The German knew he was finished now, and managed to summon a smile.

"Don't you want to hear what I had to tell you, now?" he asked Falcon.

"Speak, then, if you have no better use for your last breath." He was emptied. He'd let the man taunt him into delivering a quick death. He'd intended for it to last days.

"Listen closely, boy." Valdemar chuckled, and the blood spurted with every heave of his chest. "Your father is alive." He watched the consternation spread across Falcon's face and knew that he had had the last vengeance. "And," he said, savoring the moment, his last, "I know where he is!" He closed his eyes and died.

Falcon stood thunderstruck, his world reeling about him. If he had been able to make comparisons, it would have been the worst moment of his life since the lightning had struck him. "It can't be true," he whispered. "My father alive?"

"He lied, Draco," Wulf said. "I was there with you. We both saw Eudes. We saw what they'd done to him. What man could live more than a few minutes after that?"

"Draco," Marie said. "He just wanted to hurt you one more time before he died. But then . . ." She looked at

169

the shattered remains of the door. "But then, a thing is not impossible just because it seems so."

The chamber was dim, the candle guttering in the small pool of melted wax on its holder. Two figures lay on the tangled sheets of the bed, still but breathing heavily. After their breathing had calmed, they rolled slightly apart with the sound of damp flesh parting.

Marie stared into the obscurity of the ceiling. "Stay, Draco," she said.

"You know I cannot," he answered.

"Is your vengeance so important?" she said.

"Yes," Falcon replied. "It is. And it's more than that, now. I have to find him."

"But you know that he must be dead!" Marie protested.

"I don't know," he answered. "It's unlikely, but I'll never be able to rest until I've tracked them down and made them tell me."

"And had your vengeance," she said bitterly.

"That, too. You can never understand, Marie. You're too good and you've seen too little of what the world is like. My revenge is not mine alone. Wulf was put through the same things I was. And what they did to Father was unspeakable." At his words she remembered Valdemar's hands and his knife, and she shuddered. "But," he went on, "it's for all the others they betrayed, too. And God alone knows what foulness they've been up to since."

"Is there nothing I can offer you to keep you with me? My self you already have. I know that my father would take you as his heir. You could be lord of La Roche, one day."

Falcon gazed at her. The beautiful body was shiny with sweat, the long hair tousled. The cruel bruises were fading from her face and breast. She was indeed a prize worth keeping.

"And you?" Falcon asked. "Would you give up everything here to follow me? With your father still in captivity would you leave La Roche and all his people to follow me?"

She looked down at him a long time, then echoed his words: "You know I cannot."

A brisk early-autumn wind was blowing as Draco Falcon rode down the line of his men. The losses from the siege and storm of Pierre Noir had been replaced. Fifty men, the best anywhere. With this small band, he would build his fortune, have his vengeance, and, someday, return home and set things to rights there.

Marie waited by the castle gate, mounted on her palfrey. He had been her captain, and it would not have been fitting for him to take his leave on horseback while she stood below him. Her face was a mask of composure.

He rode up to her and removed his helmet. "My lady, I take my leave of you."

"Sir Draco," she said. "I thank you for your good service and commend you to God's keeping. I trust that you will prosper in all your undertakings."

"And I likewise wish you well, and stand ever ready to be your champion at need." They mouthed these formulas for the sake of the onlookers. They had made their own private farewells the night before with far more passion.

When all had been said, Falcon rode out through the gate with Wulf riding beside him. Behind them was Ruy Ortiz, bearing the Falcon banner, and then all the rest of the company, many of them still wearing bandages, but with all mounted nobody had to stay behind. With their job done and Thibaut dead, most of the onlookers were not unhappy to see the soldiers leave, but there were no few crying women calling for their men to come back to them.

"Where do we ride, my lord?" Wulf asked.

"Does it matter?" Falcon said. "North, I suppose. I hear that there is fighting in the north. But then, there's fighting everywhere. We won't starve."

The following is an action-packed excerpt from the next novel in this sword-swinging new Signet series set in the age of chivalry:

THE FALCON #2: THE BLACK POPE

ONE

THE mountain stream roared from the mouth of the granite-walled gorge with the bellow of an angry dragon. The winter had been hard, with heavy snows, and the spring runoff was heavy, swelling the stream to many times its normal flow. On the bank, two mounted men stared gloomily into the stream where a few jagged pilings revealed the former location of a wooden bridge.

"It must've washed out days ago." The speaker was a tall, lean man in the long-sleeved mailcoat of a knight. Just now, the coif of mail which would cover his head and face in battle hung down his back, revealing a deeply tanned face of hawklike planes and angles. His hair was jet-black except for a vivid white streak springing from the brow. From the bottom of the white blaze, a thin white line traced its way down his face and neck to disappear beneath the iron links of his hauberk.

"Shall we go downstream?" said the other man. "Maybe we'll come across another bridge." He was a few years younger than the other, and he wore a short, sleeveless jerkin of mail. Shaggy yellow locks hung from beneath his rounded steel cap.

"We've little choice," said the tall knight. "Leave a sign for the others."

The blond man-at-arms dismounted and poked about the ruins of the bridge until he found a short piece of board. This he fastened to one of the remaining piers. Apparently the bridge had been a popular campsite, and with the charred end of a stick he traced a crude but recognizable picture of a bird of prey with outstretched wings and an arrow pointing downstream. He stepped back to admire his artistry for a moment, then remounted. In silence, the two men rode, and behind them towered the magnificent peaks of the Alps, in whose foothills they had been riding for days. The region was sparsely populated, with steep, thinly soiled fields little suited for farming. Most of the people were shepherds who lived a semi-nomadic existence, following their sheep and goats from pasture to pasture. Occasionally a shepherd on a hillside would catch sight of the two horsemen, but when they sought to ask directions, the man would flee, leaving his flock and his dogs and heading for the cover of the nearest trees.

"What has the people here so frightened?" wondered the younger man.

"Who knows?" The other shrugged his massive shoulders. "It won't be the first land we've traveled through where armed men are an unwelcome sight."

At midday they came to the ruins of a village. The scene was one of utter devastation. Every house had been burned to the ground, and the ruins were still smoking. There were few bodies about, mostly those of elderly people, but all had been hideously mutilated. Even cats and dogs had been killed. The only stone building in the village was a small church, which still stood, seemingly untouched.

"Is there war hereabouts?" asked the younger man.

"This is a little thorough, even for a war," said the other. "Maybe a blood feud with another village. It looks as if all the livestock have been driven off, along with all the able-bodied men and women. Let's look in the church. If the priest lived through it he can tell us what's happened here."

"What for?" asked the younger man. "Whatever happened is none of our affair."

"I like to know who's killing whom and why, in land I'm passing through." The tall man with the white blaze dismounted and walked up the four stone steps into the church, followed by the man-at-arms. At first they could see nothing in the dim interior, but the smell that assailed them was staggering. Slowly their eyes adjusted to the dim light, and they took in the full horror of the scene. The narrow, cramped interior was crammed with bodies of men, women, and children, their corpses so mutilated that age and sex were at best matters of guesswork. The altar was so soaked with blood that it was clear that most of the butchery had been performed there. The figure of Christ had been torn from the crucifix above the altar and replaced by the body of the village priest. His genitals had been cut off and stuffed in his mouth.

Hardened warriors that they were, the two men were struck dumb by the sight. Abruptly, the taller spun on his heel and strode from the church. The other followed. They mounted and rode from the destroyed village in silence. The younger was first to speak. "I think we should wait for the others," he said. "They can't be more than an hour or two behind." His master merely grunted. "It's not blood feud, and it's not war," the young man went on. "So what is it? I've never seen anything like it."

"Don't talk like a fool, Wulf," said the other. "We've both seen worse, in Palestino and elsewhere. Acre was worse than that. So was the march through Hungary."

"It's different," the yellow-haired man maintained. "That's war between Christian and heathen. Besides, I wasn't in Hungary, though you've told me about it often enough."

"What's the difference?" said the tall man bitterly. "A synagogue full of Jews set afire or a church full of slaughtered Christians. The stink's about the same."

"But why here? This is a Christian country. Why the sacrilege and the desecration of the church? Christians kill each other readily, I'll admit, but why such butchery?"

"I intend to find out."

The sun was lowering in the west when they heard the first sounds above the roaring of the stream—the tramp of iron-shod hoofs and the clink of arms. Before them, the narrow road wound into the deep shade of a patch of forest, and it was from the woods that the sounds were coming. The knight drew the mail coif over his head and pulled its dangling veil across his mouth and nose, tying it at the temple. Now his face was completely sheathed in iron except for the pale gray eyes. From the pommel of his saddle he took a tall, pointed helmet, splendidly forged from a single piece of iron, and strapped it on. Its thick nasal bar bisected the coif's vision slit. He drew on a pair of thick black leather gloves, densely studded on their backs with pointed iron spikes. Next he took the long, triangular shield from behind his saddle and hung it by its neck strap across his back. It could be shifted to the front and his arm thrust through the arm straps in a moment. On the shield was painted a black bird of prey, clutching in its claws bolts of blue lightning. He checked to be sure that his sword was loose in its sheath and that the thong by which his ax was slung from his saddle pommel was loose and free of kinks. Satisfied with his preparations, he sat easily and awaited whatever might befall.

A file of horsemen emerged from the treeline. The

knight studied them closely, counting as they rode into view. There were seven. All were in mail. All were helmed. All bore identical black shields. Their helms and armor were likewise black. The helms were flat-topped and completely covered their faces, presenting only blank eye slits. Face-covering helms had been in use for several years, but they were still rare. The knight had never seen a whole party equipped with them. Most bizarre of all were the crests of the helms. All were adorned with horns, wings, talons, antlers, dragon spines, or other fantastic ornaments.

When they caught sight of the knight and his companion the horsemen spread out into a line abreast and walked slowly forward in ominous silence. They drew rein a few paces from the two.

"Who are you?" The voice rang hollowly from within the closed helmet.

"My name is Draco Falcon," the knight said. "Who are you?"

"Who we are is of no consequence. We have no names." The speaker wore a helm with curling ram's horns sprouting from its sides. "You are warriors, and so we must make the offer. If you wish to live, you must join us. Renounce your king or other lord. Renounce your family and renounce God. Swear fealty to our master and all we have will be yours."

"There was a village back there"—the knight jerked a thumb over his shoulder—"but no longer. Was that your doing?"

"It was. Join us and you may enjoy sport like that every day. Join or die!"

"Don't mistake us for unarmed villagers, you murdering pig!" shouted Falcon. "Out of our way or you'll be puking blood into that iron bucket!" The seven laughed maniacally.

"Kill them!" said the man with the ram's horns.

At these words, the man-at-arms kicked a leg over his saddle and landed on the ground with a small iron shield in one hand and a short curved sword in the other. At the same instant, the knight shifted his shield before his body and snatched up his ax.

A man with bat's wings on his helm couched his lance and charged Falcon. The knight shoved the lance point to the right with the edge of his shield and stood on his stirrups. The ax came whistling down, its broad blade shearing through the iron helm and stopping at the man's collarbones. Falcon dug in his spurs and his horse leaped forward, dragging the ax free with a sickening squelch. Instead of swerving to engage the next man on one side or the other, Falcon simply charged his big destrier straight into the other horse, bowling it over to send the rider sprawling on the ground. His horse sprang over the other, and then he was through the line, with Wulf running close behind. The unhorsed man scrambled to his feet, but Wulf, without breaking stride, thrust the point of his sword beneath the edge of the black helm and the man fell back, spraying blood.

Falcon wheeled his mount and faced the line of stunned horsemen. "How do you like this 'sport,' pigs?" he taunted. "A little more lively than butchering villagers, eh?" He charged the opposing line again, forcing his way between two of the riders. He blocked a sword slash from the left-hand man with his shield while ducking the sword of the other, then straightening and slamming a backhand blow of his ax into the right-hand rider's spine as he passed. Before the left-hand man could recover, Wulf was straddling the saddle behind him, one arm around the man's chest as he thrust his sword under the helm and into his neck.

"Spread out, you fools!" screamed the man with the ram's horns. The remaining three horsemen split up to give themselves more fighting room. Falcon felt a rap at his leg and looked down. Wulf was afoot again.

"I hear horsemen coming, Draco. It may be more of them. Let's ride out of here."

Falcon looked at him with rage-glazed eyes. "These swine have lived too long. I'll finish them or die myself!"

Wulf shrugged philosophically. "If you must. Take the one with the ram's horns first. He seems the most dangerous."

Falcon wheeled his mount and charged the black leader. The man with the ram's horns lowered his lance and charged in turn. The lance caught Falcon's shield dead center, slamming it back against his body and causing him to miss with the first blow of his ax. The two horses circled one another, kicking and biting. The black-armored man dropped his lance and drew sword. Falcon blocked a cut with his shield and replied with a chop that split the black shield and bit into his opponent's arm. The man howled and tried to pull free, but the ax was firmly wedged. Falcon backed his horse and hauled the other man out of his saddle. As the black horseman crashed to the ground, Falcon released the ax and drew his sword. Its blade was long, broad, and curved. Wider at the tip than at the hilt. With a backhand slash, he hewed at the neck below the edge of the black helmet. Helmet and head leaped free and the body stood for a moment as if searching for its missing parts before crashing to the ground.

"Here they come!" shouted Wulf. Falcon looked up to see the two remaining horsemen charging down on him, one from each side. If he engaged one, the other was sure to skewer him. Nevertheless, he wheeled to charge one of them. There was a faint whispering in the air, then both black riders were tumbling from their saddles, each with a yard-long shaft protruding from his mail.

Two men rode up to Falcon and Wulf. They wore no

armor, but each carried a six-foot bow. Behind them rode another twoscore horsemen. All the others were armored, armed to the teeth, and splendidly mounted.

"Gower, Rhys," Falcon said, "I thank you. They almost had me." Two more men rode up. One was a burly man with a hideously scarred face. The other was old and gray-bearded and one-eyed, with a great potbelly.

"I knew we shouldn't have let you ride ahead," said the scarred man. "You always get into trouble and have to be rescued. You've been busy, I see." He surveyed the corpses that littered the ground. He spoke with a marvelously barbarous Irish accent.

"Be these the buggers that did for that village back there?" the old man asked.

"So they said," Falcon replied. "But why, I don't know. They talked like madmen."

"Never seen anything like these turd-suckers," the old man mused. "Don't care to see any more of 'em, neither. I've been to the wars more than twoscore years, here and in Outremer, but that village back there'd make a maggot in a leper's sores puke." The old man, called Rupert Foul-Mouth for obvious reasons, was Falcon's master siege engineer.

"All armored alike, except for the horns and such," mused the scarred man, an Irishman named Donal Mac-Fergus. "What do you make of them, my lord?"

"They're a mystery to me." Falcon said. Some of his men had dismounted and were efficiently stripping the bodies of weapons and armor and clothes while others rounded up the horses. Falcon half expected them to be horned and tusked and hairy beneath the ominous black armor, but they were men like any others.

"Let's ride down out of these damned hills and find a way across this river," Falcon said. They rode away from the bloody field, leaving the seven naked bodies for whatever scavengers wanted them.

The town was not very large, but at least its people did not run away at the sight of a band of armed men. It was walled and had a spacious inn, but best of all it had a fine stone bridge. A Provencal dialect was spoken here, and the town seemed to gain its prosperity from the presence of the old stone bridge, the only reliable river crossing for many leagues. Falcon saw to the picketing of the beasts in the town common and then went with most of his men to the inn.

Many heads turned as they passed into the low-beamed common room, where welcome smells of food, wine, and ale met their nostrils. The men sat at the long benches and began calling for food and drink. Wulf helped his master divest himself of the long mail hauberk, pulling the heavy garment off as Falcon bent forward, turning the coat inside out as it rolled over his head and down his arms. Wulf carefully rolled the precious armor up, then stowed it in its oiled-leather bag. He then yanked his own mail jerkin off and dropped it unceremoniously into the straw at his feet.

The serving staff brought bread and cheeses, then sausages and meats of many kinds, all with plentiful wine and ale. The innkeeper was inquisitive.

"Are you gentlemen just returned from Outremer?" he asked between courses. "Outremer" meant "oversea," and it was the common name for the incredible kingdoms and countries the Crusaders had established from Asia Minor to Egypt.

"Some of us have been there, but not recently," Falcon said. "We're free warriors, and we fight for whoever will pay us."

"Free soldiers?" This from a man in the rich furs of a merchant, who sat across the table from Falcon. "And you hire out as a group? That I've never heard of before."

"It's been done for years in Palestine," Falcon replied.

"These men have sworn their fealty to me, and I find employment for us all. Just now we want to get across this accursed river. There's a Savoyard noble a few leagues north who wants to hire us for the siege he's laying to a kinsman's castle. We're late as it is."

"A landless lord," muttered the merchant. "How original."

Comfortably stuffed, Falcon called for one of his men to bring him one of the bags that had been propped against a wall of the common room. "Gentlemen," he addressed the merchant and innkeeper, "does this mean anything to you?" He reached into the bag and pulled out the ram's horn helm, plunking it onto the middle of the table.

The effect could not have been greater had a demon materialized on the spot. The innkeeper jumped back a yard or two, making signs against the evil eye, and the merchant turned deathly pale. All over the room, men jumped to their feet, overturning benches and spilling pitchers of wine and ale. A priest who had been eating at a far corner of the room came running over and stared with horror at the helmet, clutching his crucifix. "Where did you get this?" demanded the priest.

"From its wearer," said Falcon, mystified. "I took his head, too, but I had no use for that. There were six others and we killed them all, but there must be many more of them. They took a village two day's ride north of here and killed everyone in it. They all wore gear like this. What does it mean?"

"Bless you, my lord," the priest said. "Even if you had never gone on Crusade, killing these demons would have ensured your salvation. These monsters are the devil-worshipping followers of the heretic archbishop!"

"They've been ravaging the mountains northeast of here for months," the merchant said. "They kill all they encounter, men, women, children, taking only portable goods and livestock back to their mountain stronghold. A few have escaped, or observed them without being seen. It was from them that we learned of their black shields and armor, and the strange helms."

"They are not human," said the priest. "They are monsters and demons, shape-changers with the powers of Satan behind them."

"They were just men in outlandish gear who talked like moonstruck fools," Falcon said. "They were no harder to kill than others I've encountered."

"That is good to hear, sir," said the innkeeper. "The village you spoke of, that must be Rapides. What did you find there?" Falcon described the carnage at the village and the obscene crucifixion in the church.

"I will go to the baron myself," said the priest. "He is back from the Holy Land now and he must take action! That whole region has reeked of paganism and heresy for generations. I will demand that he mount a Crusade to clean those mountain valleys out for good!" At this there were dark looks and mutterings from the crowd assembled in the room. Neither the church nor its Crusaders were very popular in the Provençal-speaking regions.

When most of the others lay snoring in the straw, Falcon and the merchant sat up by candlelight, drinking wine and talking. The merchant made several trips each year, and Falcon wanted to know what was occurring in the north and west. He heard about Richard of England's ravagings in the north. For personal reasons, Falcon harbored a violent hatred of Richard and he made no secret of it.

"So you don't share the general admiration of the chivalrous Lion-heart?" the merchant asked.

"Richard's a bloodthirsty maniac. What he did at Acre was nothing but useless cruelty. If he's the best chivalry has to offer, then I want no part of it." Falcon stared morosely into his winecup.

"You refer to the slaughter of the prisoners. We've heard of that. So you were at the great siege, sir?"

"I was." Falcon did not tell the merchant that he had not been outside the city with the Crusader army but inside, with the Saracens.

The merchant seemed to weigh his next words carefully, but when they came they seemed to be apropos of nothing. "The winter was severe. Many of the young lambs died."

Frowning, Falcon wondered what the man was getting at. The merchant was toying idly with the hilt of his dagger, and Falcon saw that the brass pommel of the dagger was engraved with the figure of a lamb. Then he remembered. It had been the hermit in the woods last year, the one who had nursed him through his recurring fever. The man had spoken of something called the Order of Light, a band of churchmen and laypeople who were striving to bring about an end to the brutality of the times. They recognized one another through the sign of the lamb, and by speaking of "lambs and winter." From the pouch at his belt, Falcon withdrew the leaden seal from his belt and held it dangling by its thong so that the merchant could see the lamb inscribed upon it.

"I thought you might be one of us," the man said, leaning forward conspiratorially.

"Not one of you," Falcon corrected, "but I was once helped by one of your order. He gave me this and told me of your password. He had no need of my aid, but I'm a man who pays his debts."

"Then stay in this district. You heard that priest. He's going to get the baron to mount a Crusade against the heretics."

"And why not?" Falcon said. "It sounds like a fine idea to me."

"Thousands of innocent people will be slaughtered to wipe out a few score black-armored madmen. The people of those mountain valleys are harmless folk, for the most part, but they are primitive and hold to the old ways, the ancient religions. You know that to Crusaders all heretics seem alike. The bloodshed will be terrible and needless. If you and your men were to take care of the archbishop and his butchers, then there would be no need for a Crusade."

Falcon pondered this awhile. "I'm sorry," he said at length. "My first obligation is to my men, and I've contracted for them to take service with this Savoyard. Without gainful employment we all starve. I must look to their welfare first."

"That is sad news," said the merchant, downcast. "Now we must all suffer, for the Crusade will be worse than the ravages of de Beaumont's men."

Suddenly, Draco Falcon was a man transformed. He reached across the table and grasped a handful of the merchant's robe. He dragged the man bodily across the table and held the merchant's face within inches of his own. "Did you say de Beaumont?"

"Why, yes," spluttered the merchant. "That's the name of their leader, Archbishop de Beaumont." The merchant was frightened at the sudden change in his companion. Falcon released his hold, and the merchant sat heavily back on his bench.

"Tell me more," Falcon said.

"Why, there's little more to tell. The man is said to be a Fleming. He is supposed to have accompanied the Crusade, only to come back horribly changed. He was excommunicated for heresy and came into the district with his band of killers a few months ago, and set up in an ancient abbey in the mountains, near a village called Goatsfoot, where they practice their barbarous rites. Does the name mean something to you?"

Falcon said nothing for a long time. Then he took a

long swallow of his wine and smiled benignly. "Archbishop de Beaumont," he said. "I may be able to do you a service after all."

Early the next morning, the bulk of Falcon's band crossed the bridge to join the Savoyard noble, but Falcon, Wulf, and a few others headed back up the river valley, toward the village called Goatsfoot.

About the Author

MARK RAMSAY was born on St. John's Day, 1947. He is a professional writer and he lives on a remote mountaintop in the Appalachian Mountains. When not writing, he pursues his lifelong study of the Medieval and Classical periods. He makes his own weapons and armor and sometimes fights with them, when he can find someone to practice with. He feels this brings a breath of authenticity to his writing.

More SIGNET Adventure Stories